ALPHA INMATE

LILIANA CARLISLE

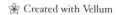 Created with Vellum

CONTENTS

AUTHOR'S NOTE

This book contains adult content not suitable for young readers. It contains explicit scenes and violence, including dramatic deaths.

PROLOGUE

ELLIE

As soon as she hears the helicopters, Ellie knows she fucked up.

They fly over her head, the sound of their blades piercing the night sky. Their lights shine down over the woods, searching for any sign of the escapee.

But they'll never find him, just like they'll never find her.

Her legs burn from running frantically in the dark. The tiny light that usually illuminates the cabin is suddenly missing, most likely from the tricks *he* pulled.

But the search lights aid her in finding refuge. The outline of her temporary residence shines in the dark and she follows it, narrowly avoiding tripping over her own feet. Her shoes *clack* against the wooden steps of the porch and sweat drips down her neck as she tries not once, but twice, to shove the key into the lock.

On the second try, she drops them.

Fighting back tears, the key finally fits into the lock, and she bursts through the door, maniacally flipping on every light switch in the front room.

None of them work, and she screams in frustration. *Of course*, he cut the power.

Slowly, the sounds of the helicopters fade away, and their searchlights dim.

Rescue isn't coming.

She can barely see through her tears, her body shaking as she fumbles around in the darkness, feeling her way towards the small kitchen. She yanks a drawer open and finds a knife, gripping the handle like a lifeline. Pushing the end of the dining table, she drags it across the wooden floor and barricades the front door. She pushes every chair against it for good measure.

He's still coming in either way, but she doesn't have to make it easy for him.

Closing the curtains and blocking out any remaining source of light, she races down to the basement, flinging the door open. She shuts it behind her, breathing heavily into the darkness. Now that the adrenaline is wearing off, every part of her aches.

Including her heart.

Her heart hurts the most, and she grits her teeth, refusing to let out the anguish that gathers in her throat.

She replays every stupid mistake she made in her mind, reliving every moment she had the chance to leave.

She had ample opportunity to escape him.

But she played right into his hands.

She can't see an inch in front of her. The darkness suffocates her, draining her of all her strength. She presses herself against the basement wall, sliding down to the floor, her head in her hands.

Her phone is dead; he made sure of it.

Just like he killed her car battery.

They should have known he wouldn't stay confined in that prison for long.

He was only there because he *wanted* to be there.

And now, he has a reason to leave.

She shivers in the dark, knife in hand, waiting for the inevitable.

CHAPTER 1

ELLIE—2 WEEKS EARLIER

"No. Absolutely not."

She caught Lita in a foul mood. Her boss looks at her with disdain, as if the very idea of Ellie's proposition is disgusting.

Regardless, Ellie presses on. "They've needed someone for a *year*," she insists, meeting Lita's scornful eyes. "They have the funding, and I'm more than qualified to do it."

She's proud of herself for not stumbling over *more than qualified*.

"No, you're not," Lita snaps, her dark eyes exasperated. "You've worked with children and students, Ellie. This is an entirely different scenario. I cannot, I *will* not sign off on this."

Her attitude only frustrates Ellie. Her temper flares, but she forces her voice to stay even. "They will only have me working with Betas, Lita. And I'm not a psychologist—I won't be doing any type of trauma work. I'm only going there to take notes, to listen—"

"It's. Not. Safe." Lita's eyes narrow, and Ellie knows the

woman won't budge. Still, she takes in a deep breath and appeals one last time.

"I can do this," she says quietly. "I know I can."

The older woman shakes her head. "So can I. It doesn't mean I *have* to," Lita insists, sitting down at her desk. She sighs, her dark brown eyes weary. "They already called me, and I told them I won't sign off on the hours. It would be pointless for you to go."

Ellie remains silent, stunned at the betrayal.

"No one is ever ready for Green Woods," Lita says softly, a hint of pity on her face. "The chip on your shoulder isn't big enough for this project. Going there won't resolve anything."

Lita's words catch her off guard and pull at something ugly in her chest.

The absolute *nerve*.

Ellie's not sure who she's angrier at—Lita for calling her out, or herself for being so transparent.

"I've agreed to a month with them," Ellie snaps, gathering her bag and standing up. "When I get back, after you see my notes, maybe you'll accept the hours."

Lita shakes her head. "I don't doubt what you do with the prisoners will be phenomenal. I'm worried about *you*. It's easy to become too emotionally involved or attached."

She scoffs at her words, frustrated that Lita could suggest that she would be less than professional. "I leave in a few days. I'll see you in a month."

Ellie hears her boss sigh as she shuts the door behind her.

———

MAYBE SHE *DOES* HAVE A CHIP ON HER SHOULDER.

Guilt gnaws at Ellie as she replays Lita's words in her head. She's opened up to the woman after knowing her for years, and her mentor knows her well.

She shouldn't have been so rude to Lita. She'll apologize later.

But on the way to the isolated town of Green Woods, she lets the worries dissipate as she takes in the scenery.

She's never seen so much greenery in her life. The trees surround her, blocking out most of the light. Her electric car had no problems in Los Angeles, but now she struggles to keep up with the twisting dirt roads and the worn-out signs. Her phone loses signal occasionally, but she navigates the directions without too much trouble.

Miles deep in dark green, Ellie begins to wonder if the place even exists before she finally sees the worn sign, the white lettering barely visible.

Green Woods. Population: 100.

"Wow," she breathes.

A building is nestled beyond a group of tall trees. Its concrete walls are dreary and industrial, nothing like the sprinkling of cabins nestled in the woods.

Green Woods Correctional Facility is a stark contrast to the surrounding nature.

Following the directions, she takes the lone road towards the cabin they've provided for her.

But as she pulls up to the dirt driveway, a chill runs down her spine.

There's a small voice that tells her maybe she should turn back, and this was a mistake.

But the stronger voice, the voice that dictates her decisions, presses on.

And so, Ellie parks in front of the cabin and makes her plans for the evening.

THIS PLACE IS NOTHING LIKE HER APARTMENT.

For one, there's no roommate. She's completely alone, with time to ruminate on her past.

There's time to relive the memories of *them* and drown in a sea of sorrow.

She shuts down the dark thoughts and unpacks instead.

The living space is furnished with a simple dining table and four wooden chairs. A dark brown sofa sits on the opposite wall, its leather frayed and worn. The kitchen is tiny, with a simple stove and fridge and only a touch of cabinet space. Her bedroom is small, with a comfortable bed and a mahogany desk.

The entire place is barely bigger than her apartment, but it's charming.

She texts Lita to let her know she's arrived safely, but the message takes thirty minutes to send due to the poor reception.

Before bed, she opens her laptop and researches more about the facility. Since its opening one hundred years ago, it's housed Alphas and Betas in different wards. Green Woods only takes inmates with crimes so heinous they could never be let back into society.

She shivers as she reads about prior cases, and Lita's words play in her head.

The chip on your shoulder isn't big enough for this project.

But she can do this. She *knows* she can.

It's only for a month. Nothing can go wrong in that short of time.

CHAPTER 2

ELLIE

SHE SLEEPS PEACEFULLY, WITH NO GHOSTS HAUNTING HER dreams.

She dresses quickly in the morning, throwing on a pair of fitted black slacks and buttoning up a cream-colored blouse. The smallest amount of eyeliner compliments her hazel eyes, and her chestnut hair is pulled into a high bun. For the final touch, she wraps a black scarf daintily around her neck, careful to cover up her mating gland.

That's the chip on her shoulder, if she's being honest.

Most people don't look at the raised bump of skin, but when they do, she hates the judgmental eyes. She's grown tired of answering the same questions.

Yes, she's an Omega. No, she's not mated.

Not that it's anyone's business.

Tying her soul to someone else is not in her best interest at the moment.

As she heads out the front door, she wonders if it will ever be.

THE DRIVE IS SO QUICK SHE COULD HAVE WALKED AND enjoyed the lush scenery, inhaling the crisp air instead of the artificial freshener in her car. Her temporary identification card allows her through the parking gate with an electronic *beep*.

She parks and stays in the car, worry gnawing at her stomach.

"What am I doing here?" she whispers to herself.

She had a plan, but now as she stares at the building, broad and overwhelming, she's starting to second-guess herself.

What is she trying to prove by coming here? That she can empathize, or somehow help unsavable monsters?

What notes would she even give back to Lita?

"Fuck it," she hisses, opening the car door.

She already came this far, she might as well follow through.

Her kitten heels *clack* against the sidewalk as she makes her way to the entrance. She slowly makes her way to the front double doors when...

Damn.

There's a scent that entices her. It's not too intense, as she has the best suppressants insurance can buy, but it's quite delicious. It's potent enough that it makes her stop in her tracks and deeply inhale the aroma.

Alpha.

Without the bustle of the city, Alpha scents don't blend into a pungent mess. This particular scent sends a thrill throughout her body, causing goosebumps to pebble on her pale flesh.

It's peppery and rich, with the slightest hint of citrus.

It's also entirely off-limits.

Get it together. You haven't even walked inside.

Well, at least she won't have to work with him. She's here for Betas only, which gives her enough reassurance to step inside.

The interior of the building is much more sophisticated than she expected. With well-lit walls and cream marble floors, it resembles more of an elite corporate office than of a prison.

It's also eerily quiet except for the throat-clearing of the guard who sits at the front desk.

Then it clicks.

This is a private facility.

Only the ones with *money* go here. Instead of landing in a public prison, their lawyers negotiated a stay here.

Interesting.

The Beta guard behind is anything but impressed as he scowls at her with beady eyes. "Yes?" he barks, his voice raspy and irritated.

Be confident, she reminds herself, standing up straighter. *You can do this.* "I'm Ellie Winters. I'm here for—"

His grey eyebrows shoot to his forehead. "They sent *you?*" he asks rudely, dumbfounded. He glances down at a paper in front of him, frowning. "No, no. We have an *Elliot* Winters."

She frowns. "No, I accepted the position here. I'm a temporary behavioral—"

"No," the guard interrupts. "Absolutely not. You can't be here."

She scowls and bites back her irritation at his dismissal. "I don't understand why—"

"Because you're—" he shakes his head and awkwardly gestures with his hands, "you're *you.*"

It's Lita's words all over again, this time with the true inflection behind it. They cut into her deeply, her heart pounding inside her chest.

Because you're an Omega.

She stands up straighter, and the same familiar anger she tampered down before returns.

"So, what's worse?" she asks him slowly. "You giving me the paperwork for *Elliot*, or me letting your manager know that you just insinuated I can't work here because of my status?"

She truly hates playing the *Omega* card.

The guard wavers for a moment, his chest heaving. Finally, his shoulders droop in defeat. "Suit yourself," he sighs. "I'll let Doctor Porter know you're here. You can take a seat, Miss Winters."

He picks up the phone and murmurs something into it, scowling.

Breathing a sigh of relief, she sits, trying her best to keep her face neutral.

She wonders if Doctor Porter will be as awful as the guard.

But a distant howl of rage and terror interrupts her thoughts. The sound ricochets off the walls; the unmistakable roar of an Alpha ringing in her ears.

She freezes.

She should have expected it—of course, there are going to be Alphas here. She already smelled one.

But the sound still chills her to her core, and she bites her lip to keep from shifting uncomfortably.

It's fine. It's fine.

The doors to a hallway swing open, and a tall, older Beta man in a white lab coat walks through them. He gives Ellie a gentle smile, and her nerves dissipate. She stands up to shake his hand, and his smile grows wider, his light green eyes crinkling at the corners.

"Ellie," he says. "I'm Doctor Porter. I hear you're working with us for the next month. I'm so sorry about the paperwork issue, by the way."

"It's fine," she says, giving him a genuine smile. "It's a pleasure to meet you. I'm looking forward to working with your Betas."

His eyes flick to her scarf, and his smile fades, recognition dawning on his face. "Oh. Maybe it wasn't clear in our communications. We offered the program for *Alpha* behavioral studies."

He thought she was a Beta. Or that Elliot Winters was a Beta.

The silence is uncomfortably long. Ellie tries to find the right words as she stands awkwardly, fighting to keep the horror from her voice.

And unmated Omega working with Alphas is unheard of, not to mention reckless.

"That's fine," she insists quickly. "I'll do it."

Her voice is two tones higher than it should be, giving away her trepidation.

But Doctor Porter isn't convinced.

"I'm sorry. I should have been clearer," he insists. "And you came all this way, too. I'm so sorry about the miscommunication."

No. *No.*

She will *not* turn around and go back home just because she doesn't want to work with Alphas.

It's *fine.* Just as she told Lita, she's more than capable. There's no law that says she can't, just the unspoken rules and social norms. But she's too stubborn to change her mind.

She forces a smile and ignores her heart pounding in her chest. "I was actually hoping to work with the Alphas, so this is a pleasant surprise."

Even the guard looks up from his desk, raising an eyebrow in disbelief.

No Omega in their right mind would do what she's offering. It's too dangerous.

It's *taboo.*

The silence is too long between them. It becomes a staring match, but Ellie refuses to back down.

"If it becomes too much, I will leave," she insists. "But I would greatly appreciate this opportunity to do research on behalf of my university."

She knows that the doctor wants to argue with her. But he won't, unless he wants to be accused of Omega discrimination.

Instead, he clears his throat and reaches over the desk for the paperwork.

"Right," he says slowly, his brow furrowing. "Okay. Well, I have you meeting with..." his voice trails off as he sighs. "Gerard, take her to Cell B."

The security guard clears his throat awkwardly, looking at the doctor in disbelief.

Ellie grows more uneasy by the minute, as both men have a silent conversation in front of her.

Something is off, she thinks.

But Gerard eventually stands up with a pair of keys, motioning for Ellie to follow.

"Before you go, Miss Winters," Doctor Porter says, "I would join you, but I have other urgent appointments. I will hold you to your word. If at any moment you're uncomfortable..."

But she flashes him a smile, proud of her victory. "Absolutely. I just appreciate the opportunity, sir."

Gerard opens the double doors, and they step inside the hall.

CHAPTER 3

ELLIE

BESIDES THE ROAR FROM EARLIER, THE BUILDING IS STILL much too quiet.

Gerard remains silent as he leads her throughout the facility, passing the overhead signs that direct to different Beta wards.

At the end of the hallway, there's a steel door. It takes a moment for Gerard to unlock it, and Ellie tries to fill the silence.

"Is the Alpha Ward this far separated from the others?" she asks.

He ignores her question.

Of course, she thinks. *You were an asshole earlier. He's not on your side.*

Her mouth made her the enemy of her only protection.

Great, Ellie.

He leads her down two dimly lit flights of stairs, walking so fast she has to rush to keep up with him.

Finally, they reach the overheard *Alpha* sign, illuminated with a faint red glow.

The only sound in the hallway is her heels hitting the floor, now concrete instead of marble.

The Alpha wing is unpleasant, to say the least.

If she was to imagine a horror movie, it would look exactly like this.

There would be nothing but concrete and silent hallways.

A haunted, dreary asylum.

"Wait here," Gerard grunts, unlocking one of the metal doors. He pulls it open, and a gust of air hits her.

Oh no.

It's the *scent.* The scent that tantalized her earlier belongs to the Alpha in Cell B.

She should end this madness now. She should turn around and run up the stairs and out of Green Woods forever. Hide back in Los Angeles, where she never has to have one-on-one time with a felon.

She doesn't even know what crimes this Alpha committed.

Would it be so bad to admit that she's not ready for this?

She hears soft murmurs from inside, then the rattling of cuffs.

No.

She's come all this way, and there's no point in backing down now.

Elizabeth Winters is not a quitter.

Gerard steps back outside, a cream-colored folder in his hands. "He's all yours," he grunts, shoving the folder into her hands. "I'll be out here. Knock when you're ready to leave. He's chained to the chair, so don't worry, *Omega.*"

He says it like a slur, and she bares her teeth, reminding herself exactly why she's staying.

"Thanks, *Beta*," she snaps, before stepping inside.

CHAPTER 4

ERIK

THE DAYS BLUR.

It's the same concrete ceilings. Concrete walls. Concrete floors.

For a while, he had his books, but Doctor Porter took them away the other day.

He ran his mouth too loudly, and apparently "upset" the other Alpha.

Well, maybe the other Alpha shouldn't have committed such heinous crimes.

All he did was remind him what a monster he was. If Kean took his own life, that's not his problem.

But now he's stuck with only a cot in one corner and a chair in the other and no reading material to pass the time.

No matter, though.

He doesn't regret what he did.

This morning was interesting, though.

Gerard, the ever-pleasant Beta, unlocked his door. "Up, Hart," he barked.

He was offered no explanation, even after he questioned the guard. And now he sits, each wrist and ankle cuffed to a chair as he wonders exactly what the hell is going on.

But the door opens, and instead of seeing Gerard again, *she* walks in.

It's such a surprise that he thinks he's hallucinating. But no, an *Omega female* enters the room, smelling like fucking heaven and looking like an angel.

Maybe they're torturing him, but he's not sure there's a crime awful enough to warrant this.

Subconsciously, he jerks against the chains, and she regards him with careful indifference, her gold eyes shining in the dim light.

He hasn't seen or smelled an Omega in three years.

He can't even think straight, as he's so dumbfounded that one would willingly come in here to talk to him.

"You must be Erik," she says, giving him a slight smile, one that doesn't reach her eyes. "I'm Ellie. I'm a behavioral analyst, and I'm here to speak with you."

It's pathetic how he's acting. Her voice, light and pleasant, sends a shock wave directly to his dick. His cock is painfully hard against his pants, and he's beyond thankful that he's sitting so she won't be able to see his embarrassing erection.

She sits across from him and puts a folder down on the desk, pulling out a piece of paper.

She's on medical-grade suppressants. He can tell that at least. Her scent is pleasant, even mouthwatering, but there's an undercurrent of chemicals that blends with it.

And she's wearing a delicate cream scarf to cover her pale neck.

Smart girl.

He comes to his senses as her eyes widen for just a moment as he notices her attire.

She's afraid.

He will not see her again after this, that's for sure. Doctor

Porter will come to his senses and drag this girl far away from here.

It's a cruelty she's inflicting on him, allowing him to bask in her presence, but then disappear forever. Soon, she'll just be a dream, a memory that tortures him for his remaining days.

Well, he can be just as cruel.

"That wasn't very smart of them." His voice, low and even, confuses her.

She licks her delicate lips and frowns. "I'm sorry?"

"Gerard can't protect you from me, little Omega."

She startles, as if slapped.

That got her.

"I don't need protecting from you, Erik," she says evenly, her face reverting to its neutral expression. "I'm actually here *for* you. To see if you're being treated properly, and if the plan of action they have for you is appropriate and not detrimental to your well-being."

He barks out a laugh.

Yes. This is definitely a cruel joke.

He shakes his head and smirks. "You're in the wrong place," he purrs. "There's no 'well-being' for me. The plan of action is to keep me here forever, beautiful."

The endearment slips out of his mouth before he can stop it, and he could swear her scent changes.

Interesting.

This is the most fun he's had in *years*.

She clicks her pen and looks down at her pile of papers. He recognizes Doctor Porter's handwriting on them, and her face slowly changes as she reads.

If he didn't know any better, he would think they didn't tell her why he's in here.

"You're in here for murder. Is that correct?"

Holy shit. They really didn't tell her.

"Is that what your notes say?" he drawls. "I would assume

so then."

She continues reading, then looks back up at him. Her light eyes have the tiniest flecks of green in them, delicate and mismatched.

They also hold the slightest bit of fear.

"You've been in here for three years. And it looks like they don't house you with other Alphas anymore."

She's doing a fantastic job of hiding her nerves, but the slight shake in her voice gives her away.

He nods. "I don't play well with others."

"I know the feeling," she mutters, and then looks up, as if surprised she spoke. "I mean, I think we've all been there."

"Have *we*?" he counters. "Tell me, where have you been, little Omega?"

He can smell her anger at his words.

She *really* doesn't enjoy being called an Omega.

Well, he doesn't enjoy temptation being handed to him on a silver platter while he's helpless and shackled to a chair.

"That scarf was clever, though. It adds a nice touch. You could almost pass for a Beta."

Her eye twitches for just a second, and he's won.

He's appalled they let her in here. That Doctor Porter could know who he is, what he's done, and still pass on that information to this Omega, and willingly let her step into this room.

And the other part of him...

"You're fucking crazy to be in here with me," he continues. "This is a pointless endeavor for you. I don't have a sob story for you, and I don't have any reason for you to advocate for me."

She bites her lip, and her brow furrows slightly as she reads. "You didn't know who these men were. You committed a random attack."

It's not an accusation. It's not even a question.

But it's inaccurate.

20

"If that's what they want to tell you, *Omega*." He smirks, enjoying their little game.

Her face turns the loveliest shade of pink as she raises her voice. "That's what I'm telling *you,* Alpha. Are they wrong?"

The anger of her scent envelops him, addicting and sweet.

Instead of answering her, he sneers. "I'm telling you, you're a stupid little girl in the wrong fucking place, *Omega*."

Her reaction is beautiful. She stands up out of the chair; the legs scraping loudly against the floor. Her temper flares, and he's overcome by the wave of emotions she's throwing at him.

"Fuck. *You*," she hisses, quiet enough that it's merely a whisper. "At least I'm not rotting in a shithole, you *monster*."

The fire in her eyes, the anger of her scent, and the soft gasp as she realizes she's lost herself is what makes everything click for him.

For the first time in a long time, he *wants*.

CHAPTER 5

ELLIE

The words leave her lips of their own accord, shattering the carefully concealed armor of her soul.

And it took less than ten minutes in a room with this monstrous man.

She should have been in control.

She *was* in control, until he threw her Omega title around carelessly, using it as the deadliest insult.

And as she towers over him, looking into deep brown eyes, she knows she fucked up.

Her reaction catches him off guard, too. She's mere inches from his face, and she's sure if Gerard looked through the door's small square window he would have pulled her out of the cell in a heartbeat.

She lost control. Not the beast in the room.

He saw through her, stabbing at her insecurities and giving voice to the doubts that were already in her mind.

Why are you here? You're not cut out for this.

There's a moment of silence too long as she studies his

face. Clean shaven, his pale face is too brutish to be pretty, and too striking to be conventionally handsome. His dark brown hair falls haphazardly, wild and unkempt. But at certain angles, he's devastatingly attractive.

And entirely too delicious smelling.

She *feels* the growl in his chest, and how it sends shivers up her spine. Her core clenches, and she takes a step back from him. As he watches her, he grins, showing bright, slightly crooked teeth.

He looks like a fucking villain.

Gathering up her papers, not saying a word, she knocks at the door.

"Goodbye, Ellie," Erik chuckles, his voice low.

Hearing him speak her name does something to her she doesn't have time to think about.

GERARD SAYS NOTHING AS HE LEADS HER OUT OF THE bottom floor, but she can see the smirk on his face.

Asshole.

"You didn't last long in there," he comments, and the arrogance in his tone makes her tense up.

"Right," she says simply. "It was a quick assessment. That's usually how my first meetings go."

Liar, she thinks. *That's never how they go.*

"So, there's going to be other meetings, then?" he asks innocently.

"Of course," she says as he leads her to the lobby. "Please tell Doctor Porter I'll be in touch."

But it's a lie.

As soon as she steps outside the double doors, she hastily walks to her car, almost losing her balance on the gravel. She slams the driver's side door shut, breathing heavily into her palms.

She can't come back here. This is way out of her league.

Erik found her insecurity much too quickly, as if he knew exactly where to dig and what words to say to unravel her.

And what was she expecting out of a meeting with him? What notes would she take?

Hi, murderer? I might be as crazy as you. Do you mind telling me why you killed those people? Do you like it here? Are the pillows soft?

Yes, I'm an Omega. And you're an Alpha. So?

And on top of that...he smells fucking delicious.

She should have worn a liner in her panties for today. They're damp with slick.

How embarrassing.

IT'S FREEZING.

She wraps herself in the blankets as she sits with her laptop on the bed, but it's not enough. The air stings, the cold so painful she's sure her entire body will turn to ice. The furnace works, but even then, the chill is persistent. So, instead of focusing on the cold, she pulls up public records to focus on the monster she met.

Erik Hart

She gasps as she looks at his mugshot. His hair is longer, falling just above his shoulders, and his eyes are dark and warm, a rich whiskey color. His face is clean shaven and pale, just as she remembers it to be.

But it's the *look* on his face that gives her pause.

It's arrogant, with no hint of remorse, with full lips pulled into a slight smirk.

Doing more research, she pulls up detailed information about his crimes.

She has to turn her laptop off, horrified at the photos.

There wasn't just one crime scene—there were many.

So many body parts in different places.

A head shoved into a mailbox. Fingers splayed out on a driveway, meticulously placed.

An eyeball glued to a ceiling fan.

No. No. No.

She was in a room with that man.

With that murderer.

The Alpha that called her beautiful.

"Holy shit," she gasps.

Lita was correct. She shouldn't have come here.

Suddenly, Los Angeles doesn't seem as dull or vapid.

She wants to drive back there and forget this ever happened, consequences be damned.

She'll run back with her tail between her legs, groveling to Lita, and it will still be better than what she just fucking saw on her computer.

There's no way in Hell she's seeing Erik Hart again.

And she hates that there's a small part of her that aches at the thought.

DARK HAIR. LARGE HANDS.

Her legs part easily for him, falling open as he takes his time exploring her.

A dark, low voice against her ear.

"You know why I did it, beautiful."

In the dream, it all makes sense.

She looks up at the ceiling fan, watching it spin around and around, a pair of watchful eyes judging them both.

"I do," she whispers back.

The fan falls. She screams.

SHE WAKES EARLY, THE SKY STILL DARK. THE BLANKETS ARE piled in a heap beneath her feet, her body soaked with sweat.

She ignores the pulsing between her legs and tries to erase the memory of the dream.

It's time to leave Green Woods forever.

She packs her stuff quickly, putting her suitcase in her car, then checks her phone. There's no signal, even though she had a bar last night.

But that's fine. She's sure she'll have reception a few miles down the road. Once she does, she'll call Doctor Porter and apologize for wasting his time.

"Okay," she breathes, shutting the driver's door. For a moment, she feels guilty, and her heart does a strange flip at never seeing Erik again.

She chastises herself, ashamed of her emotions. Is she *that* lonely and desperate for attention from an Alpha?

It doesn't matter, though. She's leaving.

But her car doesn't start.

She presses the power button over and over. She takes her foot off and on the brake, doing everything she possibly can for the damn thing to power on.

"Come on, please," she begs the electric vehicle, as if by some miracle it will listen.

It doesn't.

She puts her face in her hands and takes cleansing breaths, breathing as deeply as she can.

One. Two. Three.

She can walk to the facility and use their phone and let Doctor Porter know she will no longer be with them.

She can call a tow truck and get out of here for good.

She steps out of the car and starts the trek.

But she's not accustomed to walking in the dark and cold for long. Her puffy jacket and scarf do little to keep her body warm, and by the time she walks through the doors of Green Woods Correctional Facility, she's shivering. Gerard sits at his station and raises an eyebrow at her, annoyed.

"It's five in the morning. What are you doing here?" he barks.

Her teeth chatter. "I need to use your p-phone."

His eyes narrow, and she wants to scream at him. "No," he says simply.

"Are you serious?" she snaps, shivering. "My car broke down. I need to call a tow truck."

"It's against policy." He doesn't budge an inch, and Ellie stares at him, astounded at his audacity.

"Why do you think I'm here at five in the morning? I *walked* here."

He shrugs. "I'm not risking my job just so you can use the phone."

Her mouth falls open. "I don't understand what your problem is—"

The double doors open before she can finish her sentence, and Doctor Porter walks through, his face perking up as he sees Ellie. "Miss Winters! You're here early. But that's good," he insists. "I wanted to talk to you as soon as possible."

"Oh." Ellie stands awkwardly in front of the desk, unable to keep eye contact with the doctor's delighted expression. "I need to use your phone if that's okay—"

"Of course, but I *need* to speak with you first." Before she can reply, Doctor Porter takes her arm and leads her through the double doors and down the hallway in the opposite direction she went with Gerard. "In my office, please."

He unlocks a door, and Ellie follows him into a small welcoming room. The walls are painted light blue, with a few black and white photographs hanging from the walls. A broad mahogany desk sits in one corner, with chairs on each side. At the opposite end, facing the desk, is a black leather couch.

"Sit," he insists, taking a seat at the desk. Ellie takes the chair facing him.

She has no idea what's going on. She just needs to *get out of here.*

Erik's scent wafts into the room and she shifts uncomfortably in her seat.

"Doctor Porter," she insists, "Please—"

"It's remarkable," he says, smiling widely. "You're incredible."

That stops her.

"I'm sorry?" she asks, not sure if she's heard him correctly.

"What you've done with Erik."

Now she's *sure* she hasn't heard him correctly.

"I haven't done anything *with* him," she says, heat rising to her cheeks. "We talked for less than ten minutes. It was barely an introduction."

But the doctor's grin only grows. "He's agreed to therapy sessions with me again. He said after speaking with you, he wants to better himself."

There's a gnawing in her stomach as she remembers the smirk on his face and the cruelty in his eyes as he taunted her.

That fucking liar.

"Oh," she breathes. "That's wonderful news." She tries to sound convincing and gives the doctor a polite smile.

But I'm still leaving.

"We even spoke about his past, and he's willing to do trauma work with me," he continues. "I don't know how your conversation went, but you've done incredible, Ellie."

She laughs awkwardly. "It can't be just me, Doctor Porter. He barely knows me. I'm sure he was already making these decisions."

"I almost sent you home yesterday," he continues, and Ellie realizes he hasn't listened to her at all. "And it was wrong of me. I judged you for being an Omega, and I was frightened by what he would say or do to you. I wasn't sure you could handle it, but I was wrong. And I'm so *impressed*."

She remains silent, letting the praise wash over her, even if it's not warranted.

Erik's lying.

28

"Thank you," she says slowly. "But I'm afraid—"

"I'd like to make you a proposal," he interrupts her. "If you'd let me."

He opens a desk drawer and pulls out a piece of paper. "This is your new negotiated rate with us," he says, sliding it over to her. "If you agree to work with Erik and take him on as your patient."

She frowns and reads the paper, her jaw falling open at the number.

It's enough to buy a new electric car. Or two.

"I'm not a doctor or a therapist," she insists. "I don't have patients. All I do is ask questions about their experiences and compare them to others." She shakes her head but doesn't stop staring at the price on the paper.

"No, you're not," he says gently. "But Alpha behavior pairs very well with Alpha psychology and your notes are invaluable. I picked you for a reason to work with us, back when I thought you were *Elliot*."

She bites her lip, weighing her options. Her car is dead, her phone barely works, and Erik lied to get his way. Everything about the situation is suspicious, to say the least.

But the word "no" doesn't leave her mouth.

Instead, she picks up the pen the doctor offers her and signs her name at the bottom of her new contract.

CHAPTER 6

ERIK

SHE LEFT, YET HER SCENT STILL LINGERS.

He can smell her on his clothes.

On his fucking *skin*.

And she doesn't just smell good, she smells like *his*.

She belonged to him the moment she lost her temper and vulnerability shined in her beautiful eyes, giving him a glimpse of her soul.

Now he needs to know everything about her.

Doctor Porter practically jumped at the chance to speak with him. Erik was open and honest as they spoke, offering portions of his life he's never shared with the doctor. Of course, it's all to get *her* to stay, but Porter doesn't need to know that.

"You're too smart to be here," the doctor said to him, giving him back his books. "And something's off about *why* you're here. There's more to it than you let on."

He fought the urge to scoff. Of course, he's not telling the truth.

He'll never tell them the true reason he killed those men.

The burner phone Kean gave him weeks ago still has a little juice, and he switches it on once he's back in his cell.

There's just enough battery life to conduct some quick research.

Elizabeth Winters.

Twenty-four years old. Omega.

In moments, he finds all her public records.

Her electronic identity is bared to him, and he's able to orchestrate just enough chaos that she doesn't leave.

And, just his luck, she has an electric car.

Unlucky for her, it's easy to hack into one and render it useless.

Which is exactly what he does.

"She's agreed to work with you, as long as you continue to work with me." Doctor Porter can't contain his excitement, and it shows on his face.

And for once, he genuinely smiles back. "Sounds good."

"She'll be here tomorrow. She's getting her car fixed today."

It can't be fixed by today, he thinks.

The smile doesn't leave his face.

He can't fucking wait for tomorrow.

CHAPTER 7

ELLIE

SHE LIED TO DOCTOR PORTER.

Today isn't about fixing her car, it's about the mental preparation for what's coming.

She doesn't even bother asking Gerard to give her a ride home.

He's a prick.

Instead, she walks back to her cabin, letting the morning air kiss her skin. She breathes slowly, inhaling the crisp air and the deep, woodsy scent of Green Woods, a stark contrast from the city. Once inside her cabin, she readies for a shower.

The heat is incredible, clearing her mind and washing away the chill in her heart.

She can survive Erik Hart.

And she'll come out the other side better for it.

———

IT'S MID-AFTERNOON WHEN HER PHONE BUZZES.

She picks it up almost instantly, relieved that her signal is back, and she's able to hear a familiar voice.

"Hey," she greets Lita.

"Hi," the Beta woman says. "I'm just checking on you."

Ellie smiles, and the tension leaves her body. "Well, no one's eaten me yet, if that's what you're wondering."

She flinches at the double meaning.

Thoughts of a dark-haired head between her legs fill her mind as Lita chuckles. "No. I'm just glad you're alright. I'm going to accept those notes, you know, and add it to our research. "

Ellie fights a smile. "I know."

"I'm still pissed at you for going, but I understand why. Just be safe, please. You know Betas can be intense, even though they're not Alphas."

Her smile fades.

Lita doesn't know who she's working with.

She also doesn't know it's only *one* person she's working with, not a group.

Ellie decides not to bring it up.

"I'll keep you posted," she assures Lita. "But my reception can be spotty, so don't panic if I don't text or call you back right away."

"I'll try not to," she promises. "Also, if you need anything, or if things get too hard..."

"I know," Ellie says quickly. "They won't. But if they do, I'll come back."

"Right. I just worry about you when you're alone."

I know, she wants to say.

She bites her lip, wondering how much she should tell her. "My car broke down," she admits.

"Oh, no. Do you need me to drive up there?"

"Nah, I've got it, I promise. Everything's within walking distance."

"Alright. Well, I need to get back. I'll talk to you later, but if you need anything at all, let me know."

Her heart warms at Lita's concern for her. "Of course, I will. Bye."

She ends the call and places the phone on her bed, her head in her hands.

I worry about you when you're alone.

And with sudden clarity, Ellie realizes this is the first time she's been alone in a long time.

The fears and flashbacks threaten to take over and force her to relive the nightmare.

She stares at the cabin walls, focusing on the details of the wood, and she tries to relax.

She can't go back to that time.

She *won't.*

Once she's calmed down, she researches Erik Hart.

Going in tomorrow, she needs to prepare for what they'll talk about.

Purposely avoiding the crime scene photos, she begins to research. And the more she does, the more she's shocked at what she reads.

The man is *brilliant.*

He's the creator of security software with technology so advanced it's used by the military.

He's received numerous awards for his achievements and has been featured in different technology books and magazines.

She stares at one of the photo shoots and her mouth waters.

He's fucking *gorgeous.*

Clean shaven with his hair perfectly styled, he looks like sex personified, with his muscles on display in a fitted black shirt and dark denim jeans.

He wears the familiar smirk she saw the day before, the one that made her unexpectedly wet with slick.

But flashes of the crime scenes fill her mind.

How can that man, so carefree and handsome, commit such atrocities?

It doesn't make sense.

She digs deeper, devouring as much information as she can about him.

Both of his parents passed away years ago, with the only surviving family member being a younger sister.

She tries to piece together the clues that would finally give her the answer as to why he brutally murdered three people.

The search is fruitless, and she ends up staring at his photos, chastising herself for finding him so attractive.

It's hours later when her phone rings, buzzing on the desk. She jumps at the sudden sound.

She doesn't recognize the number, and she answers out of curiosity.

"Hello?"

"Elizabeth."

She freezes. He says her full name with such authority, his voice silky and low, that her heart threatens to beat out of her chest.

There's no mistaking who it is—Erik is calling her.

"How did you get this number?" she asks, doing her best to keep her voice even and sound professional.

"You're easy to find."

He's threatening you. End the call.

"Does Doctor Porter know you have access to a phone?" And damn it, she can't keep the waver out of her voice.

"If that makes you feel better, sure." She swears she can hear his smirk through the phone.

"If you're using an unauthorized phone, I'll have to report you."

She has no idea what she's saying, but she tries to sound convincing.

"No, you won't. Because then we wouldn't be able to talk."

Hang up hang up hang up!

"What do you want to talk about?" She squints her eyes shut, knowing this is a mistake, and grips the comforter so hard it could tear.

"I want to talk about you," he purrs, and her body flushes with heat.

"There's nothing to talk about with me," she says simply. "I'm ending this call."

He ignores her. "I'm curious why you, an Omega, think it's smart to work with someone like me. And why you agreed to come back."

She remains silent, and he chuckles.

"I don't think it's because of the money. I think it's because you feel it as well."

Her blood runs cold. "Feel what?"

He remains silent for too long, drawing out his answer on purpose to make her panic.

Hang up!

"How badly I want to fuck you."

The air leaves her lungs. Her pussy clenches at his words and her body shudders. He's right, she definitely feels it too.

"This is inappropriate," she insists, forcing herself to keep her tone even.

"Do you want me to stop? Or tell you how fucking good you smelled to me?"

Oh, God.

She's embarrassingly wet, her cunt soaking through her underwear. "Erik…"

"You smelled like sunshine and honey. Baby, you smelled like fucking *salvation*."

Oh, God.

She needs to hang up.

"Stop," she chokes out, but she doesn't end the call. His

voice is too smooth and deep for her to do anything but listen.

"You were wet when you left, like a good little Omega."

Her nipples press against her shirt, the fabric suddenly too rough against her delicate skin. She bites her lip to keep from moaning and digs her nails into the comforter.

If her car worked, she would leave right now. Damn the money. Damn it all.

"And I know you're wet right now. It's okay, baby. I won't tell."

Fuck, his *voice*.

The comforter is soaked. She bites her lip and tries her best to will herself to hang up, but she ends up gripping the phone like a lifeline.

"Do you know how hard you made me?" he continues, and she stays silent, hanging on to every word. "The hardest I've been in *years*. Do you want to know what I thought about when I made myself come?"

She can't speak. If she speaks, he wins.

Her traitorous hand moves between her legs, reaching down under her leggings, and gently rubs between her slit, teasing herself open with one finger.

Her laptop is still open, and his smirking face reflects back to her on the screen.

"I thought about splitting you open on my knot," he continues, his voice even. She works herself harder, rocking back and forth on her hand. "Thought about how that pretty pink pussy would grip me."

Her clit is throbbing. She rubs it in quick circles as he continues.

"You would fight me at first, with your pretty little self-righteousness. But I'd tie you up, baby, so you couldn't."

She grinds against her hand, so desperate and wet that tears fill her eyes.

"And if that pretty little mouth still wouldn't shut up, I'd ram my cock down it."

He just continues talking as if she knows she's close.

As if he can see her.

She accidentally lets out a choked sound, and she wants to die of shame.

He lets out a pleased hum. "You close, baby?"

And she is. She's so fucking close, and his picture stares back at her, that fucking smirk on his face...

"Come for me, Ellie. Let me hear it."

And that does it. Her body grows rigid and her pussy spasms and slick soaks her leggings. She comes thinking of his face, of his body slamming into her as he takes her cunt over and over.

She moans softly as she imagines him biting her mating gland, forcing her to be tied to him forever.

"Good girl," he praises, and she whimpers at his words. She pants into the phone, waiting for her breathing to slow.

She eventually comes down from the high and reality sets back in.

What did you do?!

He's silent on the phone as he waits for her to speak.

"That was inappropriate," she finally breathes, and he chuckles.

"Yet, you still haven't hung up."

She stares at the ceiling and thinks about what she's done, and how she has to see him tomorrow.

"Why did you kill them?" she blurts out.

Once again, he's silent for too long, and she chastises herself for being so fucking *stupid*.

"Guess you'll have to see me to find out," he says.

He ends the call.

CHAPTER 8

ERIK

HE HONESTLY THOUGHT SHE'D HANG UP ON HIM.

It was easy enough to get her number, of course. It only took a moment of glancing at Doctor Porter's notes to commit it to memory.

And when he called...

Well, he wasn't sure exactly how she'd react.

But he had to hear her voice, even if it contained the same venom she met him with the other day.

And what a fucking surprise when she stayed on the phone with him.

He wasn't lying about anything that he said. He *had* been painfully hard when she left, and he shot load after load in the cramped shower, imagining his cum dripping down her face.

But it was another experience entirely to bring her to the edge as well. When she gasped her release, it was all he could do to not growl into the phone.

She needs to show up and see him again.

If she doesn't, he won't be able to bear it.

To his surprise, it's Doctor Porter that enters the room, not Ellie.

"Good morning, Erik," he says. "We're going to my office today."

He frowns. "Why not here?"

Not that he's upset, of course. Any reason to get out of this underground hellhole and see some fucking natural light is a bonus.

"Miss. Winters requested you meet in my office."

He raises an eyebrow, surprised.

"Gerard will be right outside the door. He won't hesitate to sedate you, or worse, if you try anything."

He fights the urge to snort. Gerard is too terrified of him to do *anything*. It took one snarl and the Beta idiot had jumped backward, eyes wide with fear.

But whatever makes the doctor feel better about the decision is fine with him.

As soon as Gerard and Doctor Porter lead him up the stairs, he smells her. Her essence wafts down the hallways, and he forces himself to walk at a steady pace and not run to her.

His inner Alpha roars, excited at the idea that he'll be alone in a room with *her*.

Oh, the things he could do.

She's so tiny that she wouldn't be able to put up a fight. And if she's not wearing that stupid scarf, he'd be able to sink his teeth deep down into her.

He could claim her forever.

But he shakes those thoughts away, even as her scent grows stronger.

He doesn't want her to *hate* him. He just wants her to be consumed by him, as he is her.

That's a fair trade, he thinks.

40

But as the door to the office opens and Gerard leaves him inside, he realizes he's obsessed.

With the natural sunlight shining from the window, he can see the gold in her hair, the flush of her creamy skin, and the brightness of her eyes. She sits perched in the desk chair, dressed in a cream blouse and grey pencil skirt.

She's a fucking angel, and he's the devil.

Of course, she wears another silk scarf with her hair down, concealing that gorgeous neck.

"Ellie, Gerard will be outside if you need anything," Doctor Porter says, and he fights back a scowl. It was a warning made for him.

As if he'd ever hurt her. He only wants to give his Omega pleasure, never pain.

Well, maybe a *little* pain.

He motions towards Gerard. "What, no cuffs this time?"

"Miss. Winters requested you not be cuffed," the doctor replies evenly. "But if there's any problem, we will take the necessary measures."

Ellie's face remains impassive, but Erik raises an eyebrow at her.

Either she trusts him, or she's more insane than he is.

"Miss. Winters, are you alright?" the doctor asks.

She gives him a smile, and he feels a stab of jealousy. He wants that smile directed at him and no one else.

"Of course. Thank you again, Doctor Porter. And Gerard." She says the guard's name with just a hint of disdain, and he openly smirks.

She doesn't like him either.

Then, they shut the door, and they're alone.

Her poker face is *incredible* as she looks up at him. "Take a seat," she motions to the couch as she watches him from the desk.

He stares entirely too long at her, looming over the desk, but she meets his look with a blank one of her own.

41

Damn, she's good at hiding her emotions.

The only thing that gives her away is a subtle spike of her scent.

Satisfied that he at least has some type of reaction from her, he takes a seat on the couch and almost groans from the comfort.

"I suppose I should thank you," he starts, and her eyebrows raise. "For requesting to meet here. This is the first time I've sat somewhere relatively comfortable in a long time."

He doesn't miss the frown as she jots down a few words in a notebook. "Well, I'm glad I could help with your comfort."

She doesn't sound glad at all. In fact, there's no mistaking the fire in her eyes as she looks back up at him.

"I'm glad I could help you with *your* comfort as well," he purrs, and her scent intensifies with her anger.

It's delicious. It's darker, like bittersweet chocolate.

"I don't know what you're talking about," she says evenly, and he scoffs.

"Oh, sweetheart, are we both going to lie to each other? I thought we got along pretty well last night."

He doesn't miss how she squirms in her seat. "Erik, I'm here to talk about—"

"Don't lie to me, *Miss Winters*," he purrs. "And I won't lie to you."

She puts her pen down and sighs, looking up from her notes. "Alright," she says quietly. "But I will say, last night was a mistake and something I will never do again. I could lose my job. I *deserve* to lose my job."

He remains silent, and she continues.

"But two days ago, you asked me why I was here. I came here originally to work with Betas. I study the class differences between Alphas, Betas, Omegas, and their life experiences. Usually, I work with youth. This was my first assignment to a place like Green Woods."

Interesting.

"So why me?" he asks incredulously. "If you were working with children, why assign yourself to an Alpha inmate?"

She looks away and sighs. "It was an accident," she says quietly. "There was a miscommunication, and I ended up assigned to you."

There's a moment of silence as she stares at her notes, refusing to meet his eyes.

"You could leave," he goads. "You could quit now."

But he knows she can't leave.

He made sure of it.

She clucks her tongue and shakes her head. "I don't like to make a habit of quitting things. We've already made it this far. Why not go all the way?"

She realizes her wording, and she blushes. It makes him laugh, and she clears her throat.

"But I do have questions for you, which I should have asked you the first day I was here," she continues. "And I owe you an apology for my reaction. It was uncalled for."

"There are better ways to apologize, sweetheart," he purrs, and the blush grows on her face. "But I suppose for now, this is fine."

She rolls her eyes, and he finds himself enraptured as she continues. "I have questions if you're willing to answer them. If not, I can just leave for the day, and we'll try again tomorrow."

Fuck that.

He'll sing like a canary and tell her every depraved thought he's ever had if he could inhale her scent for just another minute.

"Fine." He agrees. "Fire away."

"Do you think you're treated differently here as an Alpha?"

She can't be serious. The question is ridiculous. He almost

scoffs at her, but he sees the earnestness in her eyes and the eagerness to learn what she can.

And as impossible as she is, she's also endearing.

"Of course. There isn't even a question," he deadpans. She nods while scribbling down a few notes.

"Can you give some examples?"

His temper flares to life, and he wants to scream.

Well, for one, I'm completely obsessed with the Omega across the room from me.

"I'm pumped full of suppressants against my will."

She stops writing, and a confused expression crosses her face. "What do you mean?"

"Well, sweetheart," he says, relaxing on the couch, and spreading his arms across the back of it. "Every morning, your doctor buddy jabs me full of a military-grade suppressant. Which I never asked for."

He can practically see the wheels turning in her head. There's horror on her face as she realizes how unethical the act is. Suppressants are always voluntary, even if most Alphas and Omegas choose to take them. But forcing them upon someone is inhumane.

But the clever girl she is, she doesn't take the bait and question him. Instead, she smooths her emotions back, putting on the same professional mask as before.

"Any other differences?"

Her scent dances around him, speaking to his inner Alpha, and he smiles at her. "I don't want to take them. They make me a little...off. Make me see things. Maybe do things I don't want to do."

He's toying with her, and it works. That beautiful whiff of her fear speaks directly to his cock. And God, does he enjoy playing this game with her.

It's too much fun to torture her with words.

She clears her throat. "Does the Doctor know this?"

44

But he rolls up his sleeve, ignoring her question. "See this?" He points at a round raised patch of red skin at the top of his forearm. "Gerard gave me that. He's not the biggest fan of me. But I'm assuming he doesn't like you, either, since he willingly locked you in a room with me."

She pauses. "We're not locked in," she breathes, glancing at the door.

He follows her gaze and smiles when he sees Gerard is missing from his post.

CHAPTER 9

ELLIE

SHE'S LOCKED IN HERE WITH HIM.

She smells his triumph, possessiveness, and lust as he grins.

"I'm sure he'll claim it was a mistake later," he says. "But I think Porter had him do it to test me."

None of this makes sense. He has to be lying.

"How do you know the door is locked?" she asks, feigning indifference, her eyes still searching for Gerard's face through the small window.

He's not there.

And Erik just sits on the couch, sprawled out and smiling like the cat who got the cream.

"He locked it when he closed the door, which I thought was odd. My week's been full of surprises."

Her heart beats so hard in her chest she's sure she'll die.

He's only moments away from her if he stands up. It would take two long strides before she would be in his arms and his to take or tear limb from limb.

He wouldn't do that, her inner Omega voice insists. *He wouldn't hurt you.*

Wouldn't he, though? He dismembered three people and didn't show remorse.

He tilts his head and gives her a crooked smile as he lounges on the couch without a care in the world.

She's going to throw up.

The dynamic has changed. He's in control, and they both know it.

"You could always try the door, if you don't believe me," he says casually. "But I believe we have an hour until our session is over, and I wouldn't want to waste precious time."

He's teasing her.

But reminding herself of who she is and why she's at Green Woods, she nods. "I suppose you're right. And we do have more things to talk about."

Instead of finding disappointment on his face for refusing to play his game, he looks impressed, and he gives her a genuine smile that steals her breath. "Ask away, Miss Winters. I'm suddenly in a very talkative mood."

She glances back at her notes and says what was gnawing at her gut. "I'm sorry about the suppressants," she says genuinely. "If you like, I could talk to Doctor Porter, or even write up a report based on what you told me."

His smile fades, and he sits up straight. "Ellie," he murmurs, and his voice sends a chill down her spine. "They do it for a reason. I'm a criminal. It's what I deserve."

He states it factually, without a trace of self-pity in his tone.

It's not right, she wants to insist, but then she remembers where she is.

This is not a foster home or a high school.

She's locked in a room with a man deemed too dangerous for society.

Now is not the time to be a bleeding heart.

She needs to run out the clock, hoping that either Gerard or Doctor Porter will show up once their hour is complete.

"Right. So—"

"You have a problem with being called an Omega," Erik interrupts, and she freezes.

He's not wrong.

"I disagree," she says calmly, even though she's panicking on the inside.

"I said it twice to you, rather rudely," he admits, "but I never expected you to react the way you did. Something about being an Omega upsets you."

"We're here to talk about you," she snaps, and he gives her that brilliant smile again.

He found the chink in her armor.

"There's nothing wrong with who you are," he says slowly, his eyes burning into hers. "You're brilliant. Beautiful. Everything an Omega should be."

His voice sounds like honey, the words falling perfectly from his plush lips, but she knows she can't give in to this.

Even though he's said the words she's longed to hear from basically...anyone.

You know he's a liar, a voice inside whispers. *If he knew what you've done...*

And that's part of what makes her so angry.

Even if he meant the words, they're not true. They could never be true.

"I'm asking you, respectfully, to please stop talking about this."

She expects him to laugh at her and keep going. Instead, he narrows his eyes and sighs.

"Alright," he says, after a long pause. "Okay."

"Thank you," she replies, and she almost laughs at the absurdity of *her* thanking *him* for not harassing her.

Their dynamic is dangerous.

She needs Gerard to *unlock the fucking door*.

The longer she spends in the room with this man, the longer she wants...

Him.

Her inner Omega fights with her, demanding she move closer to him. Even in his prison scrubs, a dark blue cotton shirt, and pants, he's still disturbingly attractive.

And his scent is *phenomenal.*

The longer they're in the confined space, the stronger his scent caresses her. She wishes she could bottle up that scent, spray it all over herself back at the cabin, and...

No.

"You asked me why I did it last night," he says suddenly, and her eyes widen. "I'm sure you've seen in my file that it was a random act."

She nods slowly, hanging on his every word.

"It wasn't, Ellie."

She holds her breath, her pen trembling in her hand.

"It was revenge."

There's too long of a pause as they sit there in silence, his eyes never leaving hers.

He's telling the truth. She can practically feel it in her bones, but the pen in her hand stays frozen in place. "You don't have to say any of this to me," she whispers. "It would be better if you told Doctor Porter instead."

"You're the only one I want to tell," he whispers, leaning forward on the couch. "I have a feeling that maybe you, of all people, might understand."

It's a ridiculous notion. She could never, ever understand what he did. How he could dismember three different men and dispose of their bodies in horrific ways.

It was revenge.

What does she know about revenge? Nothing. She's never taken revenge on anybody. And even if she could...

If there was one person she could take revenge on...

Oh.

And suddenly, that festering, tiny little voice in the back of her mind screams in agreement.

Yes, she could know a lot about revenge if she tried.

If I could, I would.

"I understand," she whispers, shocking both of them.

CHAPTER 10

ERIK

THE GIRL'S FUCKING CRAZIER THAN HE IS.

Not only does she not hysterically bang on the door, but she also doesn't even try to see if it's locked.

She just takes his word for it.

And then,

"I understand."

Her mouth forms a small 'o' as the words leave her, and he's dumbfounded into silence as well.

He didn't expect her response. He doesn't even know why he shared with her part of the truth, except that it felt right after she'd been so vulnerable with him.

After she was so brave.

And now, his little Omega is more twisted than he thought.

She's a puzzle, his girl. She's more layered and complex than he imagined.

It's a shame she doesn't know she's already his.

She sold her soul to him when she came apart on the phone as she breathed his name while coming on her fingers.

But he needs to bide his time and strike when the timing is right. He needs her to trust him.

He needs...

Beep. Beep. Beep.

An obnoxious alarm goes off, so loud they both jump.

Beep. Beep. Beep.

They stand up at the same time, and her scent *spikes* with fear as she tries the door, yanking on the metal handle desperately.

"What the fuck?!" she hisses as she acts like a madwoman, throwing her body weight against the door. The door is locked, just like he suspected, and her panic grows.

Beep. Beep. Beep.

"It's just the fire alarm," he says evenly, taking another step towards her.

She turns to him and blinks back tears, her face red with exertion. Her fearful eyes stare at him, horrified.

Beep. Beep. Beep.

Her reaction is so unexpected that he blurts out what he thinks are reassuring words.

"We're not going to burn to death, don't worry."

That was the wrong thing to say.

Her body grows rigid as she stares at him in fear, her hand gripping the door handle so tightly that her knuckles turn white.

She's stopped breathing.

What he wouldn't give to look inside that pretty little head of hers.

He takes another step towards her. "Ellie, it's alright," he assures her softly, as the alarm fills the room. He's never been this close to her before, and he towers over her delicate body. Her scent washes over him, calling directly to his cock.

Beep. Beep. Beep.

52

Gerard should be at the door by now. The window on the other wall isn't big enough for Erik to climb through, but maybe if he breaks it for her, she can get out.

He'll do anything to get that look of panic off her face.

He reaches out and takes her hand, her skin hot and clammy against his. Her eyes widen as he grips her hand tightly, trying to offer reassurance.

She's never going to see him after this.

This time, he knows for sure.

And if Gerard comes in right now, and sees him touching her...

Well, fuck it.

What he's about to do is unthinkable, but he can't deny he's wanted to do it since he first laid eyes on her.

"*Omega. Look at me.*"

His powerful Alpha Influence washes over her easily in her moment of vulnerability. Her pupils grow so wide her eyes are almost black, but her body relaxes.

"*Calm down,*" he breathes to her, sending his Influence as deeply as he can. "*You're safe.*"

Beep. Beep. Beep.

Her face is still flushed, but her breathing evens out as she looks up at him with wonder.

And it's wrong to want to touch her like this when she can't resist. He could command her to do anything he wanted.

But not like this.

He lets go of her hand, just as he hears footsteps coming down the hall.

He only has moments before Gerard opens the door.

Beep. Beep. Beep.

But still...

His hand quickly reaches out and wraps around her waist, pulling her towards him. He lowers his head and presses his lips to hers gently, her essence filling his senses. She gasps

53

against his mouth and her hands automatically grab at his shirt.

He suppresses a groan as he tastes her, before finally pulling away and taking steps back.

She's fucking heaven on his tongue, just like he knew she would be.

Beep. Beep. Beep.

"Ellie," he says, and she snaps out of her stupor. Her eyes are wide and her fingers go to her mouth as if she can't believe what just happened.

Keys jangle against the lock.

"Don't run from me. You're showing up tomorrow."

Gerard opens the door and ushers her out.

She doesn't look behind her.

CHAPTER 11

ELLIE

HE *KISSED* HER.

Beep. Beep. Beep.

He used his Influence to calm her, and then kissed her. His lips were impossibly soft against her, and she could have drowned in his kiss forever.

It infuriates her. She decides to take it out on Gerard.

"Where *were* you?" she screeches, running to catch up with his strides. "Why weren't you outside the door?!"

"Away," he says simply, walking down the hallway.

Beep. Beep. Beep.

She sputters, enraged at his attitude. "What is wrong with you? What if he had attacked me?"

He chuckles as he leads her down the hallway. "I highly doubt that. Besides, it's not like you'd say no."

"*What?*" she shouts.

Beep. Beep. Beep.

But Gerard ignores her and continues walking.

They meet Doctor Porter at the front of the building just as the fire alarm stops.

"Miss Winters!" he exclaims, waving a hand at her. "It was a false alarm! I apologize." He frowns and looks at Gerard. "Is Erik..."

"He's still in your office," Gerard says. "Locked in."

The Doctor nods. "Alright. Bring him to his cell."

Gerard walks away, leaving Ellie with Doctor Porter.

"Are you alright?" He asks her, and it takes a moment to pull herself together.

There's no fire.

Erik kissed me.

She nods, flashing him a small smile. "Absolutely. We were wrapping up, anyway."

Liar.

"Well, I look forward to discussing your session with him. Let's meet tomorrow morning?"

She nods hurriedly, walking towards the door. "Of course."

"Look for an email from me tonight. I'm so sorry about that alarm again. You look a bit spooked."

She barks out a fake laugh. "Just a little jumpy today. Too much coffee."

She lets the door fall shut behind her before she can engage with the doctor again.

IT'S COLDER THAN LAST TIME.

Something tells her she shouldn't be walking in this much snow and cold, but she needs to burn off her anxious energy.

Her breath comes in short clouds in front of her face as she walks, the cabin coming closer into view.

There are too many things to process.

Erik fucking *kissed* her.

He kissed her, after using his Influence to calm her.

56

Part of her is furious.

How *dare* he reduce her to nothing but a submissive creature?

But she never felt as safe as she did at that moment. His touch was a soothing balm to her soul and quieted the fears and flashbacks brought to life by the fire alarm.

And his sinful lips were too soft and full for their own good.

No.

She's already shared too much with him. He knows too much about who she is, about her empathy towards revenge and her absolute meltdown over something as simple as a fire alarm.

This is over. It has to end.

But apparently, fate has other plans.

"I'm sorry, Miss Winters, but no one can come in or out of Green Woods because of the storm on the roads."

She clenches her teeth as she tries to reason with the towing company. "I will pay whatever you need. I just need *someone* to get me out of here. Please."

"I'm sorry, ma'am," the receptionist sounds truly sympathetic. "But it will be at least another few days before anyone can tow you. No cars are coming in or out."

This is a joke, she thinks. *A cruel fucking joke.*

She ends the call, and her phone buzzes almost immediately.

It's a private number.

She powers off her phone, not wanting to deal with whatever *he* has to say.

The entire trip has been a mistake, for so many reasons.

His words from before fill her mind, the ones he spoke right after he kissed her.

Don't run from me.

But she *should* run. She should get as far away as she can from Erik and Green Woods.

She could forget it all, pretend it was a nightmare, and go back to working in Los Angeles.

Yet now, she can't even leave. She's snowed in.

Trapped.

It's been less than a week and he's seen more of her than most people have in the last few years. Only Lita knows about her fear of fire, yet she showed her vulnerabilities within three days of meeting the murderous Alpha.

And at that moment, she had wanted to tell him everything.

She wanted to tell him that in the darkest parts of her soul, she believes that revenge is the answer.

And that truth scared her more than she could imagine.

She *should* quit.

But her inner Omega knows she won't.

———

She's upside down, blood rushing to her ears as smoke burns her lung.

Mom doesn't make a sound. Neither does Juliet.

She hopes it's because they made it out of the car.

Fumbling, she reaches for the latch on her seatbelt, pressing the button until she falls out of her seat.

Her body screams with pain as her hands find gravel. She pushes on, shoving herself through the small opening of twisted metal. Glass embeds in her palm as painful splinters, but she forces herself to keep going.

Her leg catches on something sharp. She cries out, kicking furiously at the stinging sensation, until her pant leg rips and she's out of the car.

The air tastes of rubber. She dry heaves, smoke burning her eyes and filling her nostrils.

There are shouts, with rough hands dragging her away until finally she breathes fresh air.

She stares at the car, now just a smoking heap, and a horrible realization hits her.

They're still inside.

SHE WAKES UP WITH A START, SOAKED IN SWEAT.

Her body shakes, and she wraps her arms around her knees, rocking back and forth.

You can't change what happened, she thinks to herself.

The past is the past.

But her fear of fire triggered one of the worst nightmares she's had.

Jumping out of bed, she flips on all the nights, too wired to go back to sleep. It's barely even morning, the sun only beginning to creep in through the window.

She grabs her phone and reads the email Doctor Porter sent to confirm their meeting.

He kindly offered to pick her up, but she groans at the thought. She's not sure she can look him in the eyes ever again after Erik kissed her.

She should quit, regardless of the money. All of this is madness, and it's gone too far.

But...

Now she doesn't want to.

She wants more of the taste of Erik's lips and the feeling of his inner Alpha speaking directly to her Omega.

If she's honest with herself, it was the best kiss of her life.

It was sweet and chaste with the promise of passion.

Don't think about him. It's inappropriate.

Oh, but how she wants to.

She wants to think about the massive size of his powerful

hands and the way they could wrap around her waist easily to lift her against a wall.

She wants to think about his mouth at her mating gland, the one she tries so desperately to hide behind her hair or scarf.

She wants to think about how it would feel to give in to her desires.

You need to stop.

She opens her laptop to study more about his heinous acts, desperate for anything to snap her back to reality.

She looks at the crime scene photos again—this time, through a different perspective.

Revenge.

What could these three men have done to warrant that brutality?

Erik not only tortured the victims, but he also antagonized their families.

One of the Alphas he killed was married, and he sent a finger of the man to his wife, the wedding ring still attached.

She stares at each photo and reads each file, trying to put the pieces together.

There was no evidence linking him to the crimes—he executed them perfectly.

He wasn't even a suspect until...

He turned himself in.

Her mouth falls open in shock.

THE COFFEE SHOP IS BARELY A MILE FROM THE FACILITY, and Ellie couldn't be happier to smell the familiar scent of roasted beans.

"Do you have everything you need for the rest of your stay here?" Doctor Porter asks her, sipping his cappuccino.

"The storm is going to make everything much more difficult. Does your car have chains on the tires?"

She frowns. "Actually, the battery in my car died. I've been walking to the facility every day."

His grey eyebrows shoot up. "Absolutely not! I'll make sure Gerard picks you up in the mornings and takes you home as well."

She shakes her head. "No, really, it's fine—"

"Ellie." The doctor says gently, his eyes kind. "A Los Angeles winter differs greatly from a Green Woods winter. You're not walking in that mess. You'll blow away in the wind or freeze to death."

She wants to protest, but the doctor is right. His concern for her well-being tugs at her heart, and she nods. As much as she doesn't want to ride with Gerard, she also doesn't want to butt heads with the person she's working under.

"Alright," she agrees. "Until I can finally get my car working again after the storm."

"Perfect!" he exclaims, opening his notebook. "Now, let's discuss my favorite patient."

"Oh," Ellie says, hastily putting her cup down and opening her laptop. "He's your favorite? Of everyone?"

"Maybe *favorite's* not the right word," he corrects himself, but continues to smile. "But he is by far the smartest and most interesting resident of Green Woods Facility."

Ellie nods, keeping her expression neutral. "He's not what I expected."

"And before we go further, I owe you an apology, Ellie."

His words surprise her. "Why?" she asks, confused.

The doctor clears his throat and shifts uncomfortably. "I judged you for your...status," he confesses. "I was nervous about you working with Erik. And I can see I was wrong. I'm very sorry, Miss Winters."

She shakes her head. "You already apologized before. It's fine—"

"No, it's not. I had an unconscious bias because you're an Omega. I'm very embarrassed and truly sorry."

She nods. "Thank you," she whispers.

"And Erik...he can be difficult," he adds, frowning. "He can easily use his words as weapons, and they have serious consequences. That's why I told you the minute you became uncomfortable, leave."

A chill runs up her spine because the doctor is correct.

Erik made her fall apart on the phone with only his words.

But she changes the subject before she follows that train of thought. "Why is he the only Alpha here? Is that normal? You have an entire ward dedicated to them, right?"

There's a moment of silence before he speaks. "Well, there was another Alpha here. But unfortunately, he died while in our care."

"*Oh*," she says awkwardly. "That's terrible."

He sighs. "Remember how I said Erik can use words as weapons? He was within earshot of Kean for a while. And Erik didn't like him at all."

A wave of nausea overtakes her, and she has a feeling she knows where the story is headed. "I see."

"We believe Erik convinced him to take his own life."

It's like a cold slap in the face.

All the attraction she felt towards the Alpha evaporates into guilt and horror.

"We moved him to a soundproof, isolated cell after that," Doctor Porter continues in a somber voice.

Ellie stares at the table, refusing the look the doctor in the eyes. "What was Kean in there for?" she asks, her voice barely above a whisper.

"He was a serial rapist."

Revenge.

"He seems to have a vigilante complex," the doctor says.

"He's never told me, but I believe the murders he committed weren't random."

"He turned himself in," Ellie adds. "They had no reason to suspect him."

"Right," he agrees. "Something doesn't add up, and even though it's not my place, I know he has a story to tell. And maybe he will if the time ever comes."

Revenge. He did it for revenge.

She swallows, and even though it feels like a betrayal to Erik, she offers what she knows.

"When I was speaking to him, he alluded that there was a reason for what he did," she says softly.

Doctor Porter gives her a small smile. "Maybe. Or perhaps I'm finding false hope in someone who can never be redeemed."

Me too, she thinks.

They still have more to discuss, though.

There's a pressing issue in the back of her mind.

"I also had a concern, which I would like to go over with you. Is he being administered suppressants against his will?"

To her surprise, the doctor nods. "Yes. To keep everyone else safe."

She frowns. "Even though you only have Betas and Alphas in your facility?"

"An Alpha in Rut can overpower any Beta if they choose," he says slowly, staring at her as if the reason is obvious. "It's not safe."

She remains silent, not wanting to push the issue—but it raises a red flag.

Not that she *wants* him to go into a Rut, but it should be Erik's choice.

She files the information away in her head to report back to Lita.

But to her surprise, Doctor Porter sympathizes. "I know what you're thinking, Ellie," he says. "And I don't necessarily like it, but he's never voiced his concerns to me. Sometimes, you have to do the wrong thing for the greater good."

Something uncomfortable stirs in her and she quickly changes the subject.

"Has any family come to visit him?" she asks. "I know he has a sister."

He raises his eyebrows. "Oh. I'm surprised you don't know. His sister passed away a few months before he came here."

She gasps.

He knows what it's like; she thinks. *He knows the pain.*

"That's awful," she whispers, as the doctor nods.

"It is. And to answer your question, no family visits—he doesn't have any, really. The only people he speaks with are me, Gerard, and now you."

She has no response to that.

"He's here for the rest of his life, longer than I'll be alive. Longer than you'll be here, for sure. And a small part of me pities him." He shakes his head, his face overcome with misery.

"Why would you pity him?"

"He's a brilliant man, Ellie," he says. "Insanely intelligent. He designed the security system we used to use. We had to install a whole new program when he arrived."

A chill runs down her spine as he continues.

"He threw his life away for reasons he won't share. He's doomed to rot here, with only myself, Gerard, and now you as company. Eventually, everyone will forget him."

Tears prick at her eyes and she does her best to hide them.

"He'll never have a mate, either. Without a mate for an Alpha...I fear if he's not already unstable, it's only a matter of time before he truly falls into madness."

She can barely keep her hands from shaking as she asks

her next question. "What about the other Alphas you had here? Did the same thing happen to them?"

He nods slowly, sorrow etched on his face. "That's why we eventually made the suppressant injection mandatory. No matter how much of a monster someone may be, the sounds of a man howling with loneliness still hurt to hear."

Her chest aches as she imagines Erik howling from loneliness.

"You're far more empathetic than me," Ellie tries, giving him a small smile.

He shrugs. "Not always. With Erik, I have a soft spot. And now I have one for you, too." He takes a sip of his drink, his eyes warm. "Whatever you're doing with him, keep doing it. I would like to improve how this place runs when treating Alphas. Whatever information or ideas you have, please pass them on to me."

"I will, Doctor. So far, it was just about the suppressants. I'm glad I understand why, even if I don't agree."

"You're doing a great job, Ellie. I'm extremely impressed."

And as much as she would like to bask in the praise, guilt stands in the way.

The phone call.

The kiss.

She was supposed to tell Doctor Porter about how Gerard locked them in the room, yet she can't bring herself to do it.

Part of her *liked* it.

And that's what scares her.

CHAPTER 12

ERIK

She doesn't come for two days.

For *two fucking days.*

"She'll be back tomorrow," Doctor Porter says after their session, as if reading his mind. "She's reviewing some notes back at the cabin."

If the doctor realizes he made a mistake, he doesn't show it.

So *that's* where she is.

It makes sense. The nearest hotel is around twenty miles away, and if she's planning on staying longer than a few days, the hospital saves money by keeping her at their cabin instead.

As he's lost in thought, a knowing look shines in the doctor's eyes.

"You like her."

He says it matter-of-factly, almost smugly, and he wants to punch him right in his grinning face.

66

"She's decent," he offers. "She's intelligent and seems interested in what happens here."

She's everything.

"She brings something to this place that was missing." The doctor chuckles to himself. "I'm not sure what...but she's making my job easier. We had a great coffee date."

He says it so wistfully that if he wasn't a Beta, Erik would attack him. Still, he feels a stab of jealousy as he imagines Ellie sipping coffee and chatting politely with Doctor Porter.

His chest vibrates, a low growl rising in his throat, but the doctor doesn't notice.

"If you keep working with me, we can add outdoor time, as well as other privileges. It will have to be after the storm, though. According to the weather reports, this one is going to be nasty."

There's only been one other major storm since he's been here. That time, the power shut off, and the generators were the only things keeping the doors locked.

He wonders what this storm will bring.

HE'S PAINFULLY HARD, AND ALL HE CAN THINK ABOUT IS *her*. She's a poison in his mind, a parasite embedded so deeply in his brain that he'll never be the same.

He pulls out his hidden phone, now fully charged. Porter was so oblivious as Erik opened up about his life that he didn't see the tiny green light under the couch, the phone battery charging in the outlet covered by the back of the couch.

He needs to know *everything* about her.

Omega Omega Omega

Need Omega

His brain is haywire, the thought of her consuming his mind and body.

He types out a message before he can stop.

Do you know how fucking beautiful you are?

He waits patiently for a response, knowing that she read the message.

Stop, please.

He can't. A better man would leave her the fuck alone and report his sins, so she would be safe from him forever.

A good man would tell Doctor Porter that she's not working out for him and it's better that she leave.

Too bad he's no longer a good man.

He was once, a long time ago.

But that man is gone.

You tasted so fucking good on my tongue, Omega. You were such a good girl.

She read the message.

No response.

He continues.

Do you know what good girls get? Good girls get fucked. Good girls get their cunts licked and their clits sucked until they come all over my face.

Message read.

No response.

I know you're wet for me. Play with your clit, baby. No one has to know.

Message read.

He palms his cock through his pants, squeezing the girth and imagining her mouth around him.

Wish I was there, baby. I would lick you clean and stretch you open with my fingers. You'd be so fucking tight for me.

Message read.

And he just knows, every part of him *knows* she's touching herself right now. He can practically hear the cadence of her breath, the sound of her gasping against her own fingers as her slick stains the sheets of the bed in her cabin.

He squeezes himself harder, one hand working his cock while the other types.

I want to knot you so fucking bad, Ellie.

Message read.

Split you open. Make you come all over my cock like a good girl.

Message read.

Are you touching yourself, Omega?

If she has any sanity, any reason within her, she will turn off her phone and run far, far away.

Message read.

Then she responds.

Yes.

It's one sweet, simple word, but he growls, working himself harder.

Fuck. What he wouldn't give to smell her in this instant, to put his lips against the delicate gland she hides so discreetly—

Make yourself come.

Message read.

He finishes in his hand, his seed spurting all over his hands and stomach.

Still, it's not enough.

He needs to be *buried* in her cunt, feel her delicate walls squeezing him as she rides his cock, only stopping when he inflates too wide inside her.

As he collapses on the small cot, he wonders if his suppressants are working as they should.

He wonders if *hers* are working.

CHAPTER 13

ELLIE

IT'S OFFICIAL.

She's a whore.

She washes the slick off her hands then takes an impossibly hot shower, trying to wash away the shame and arousal that courses through her.

How could she? It's a question that rattles around in her mind as she shampoos her scalp, scrubbing harder than necessary.

What the fuck is she *doing?*

She spent the day planning out her next time with Erik and the questions she would ask, typing up notes and observations for Lita...

But then she spends her night spreading her legs to his text messages, sent from a phone he shouldn't even have.

And it feels so fucking *good.*

Even as she stands in the shower, slick still dribbles out of her, her cunt over sensitized. Her nipples ache, so sensitive that the slightest touch makes her clit throb.

She squeezes her eyes shut and allows her mind to wander, to wish for just a moment that the person who she feels closest to isn't an inmate with a lifelong sentence.

But it's too late.

She wants him.

He wants her.

And she's unable to leave Green Woods.

As if on cue, thunder booms as she steps out of the shower, wrapping herself in a fluffy towel.

The fabric feels incredible against her skin, so she wraps herself in another.

Then another.

But she wants more.

"Oh!" she gasps, as she opens the closet door to find extra blankets. She throws them on the bed, her inner Omega rejoicing as she lies down in the fabrics.

She sighs into her makeshift nest, burying herself under blankets and thinking of Erik's handsome face.

Snap out of it, her rational mind snaps, but her inner Omega wins the battle.

Just for tonight, it begs. *Let's think about him just for tonight.*

"Just for tonight," she murmurs.

Her inner Omega rejoices.

GERARD PICKS HER UP IN THE MORNING.

She wants to protest, but she knows she wouldn't last ten minutes in the cold. The sky is a violent dark grey, and she's outside mere moments before goosebumps prickle on her skin.

He barely glances at her as she enters his car, murmuring a 'thanks' as she shuts the door.

It's unpleasant. This close, he stinks of cigarettes and sweat, and she does her best to not show her disgust.

They ride in silence. When they arrive at the facility, he gets out of his car and walks purposely ahead of her.

Asshole, she thinks, shivering as she enters the building. She greets Doctor Porter with a smile, who immediately looks concerned.

"Are you alright? Your face is a bit flushed."

She swears he can see through her and that he knows his star pupil has been committing unspeakable acts with his favorite patient.

"I'm fine." She lies easily, the words spilling from her mouth without a second thought. "Just cold."

But despite the chill, her body has been uncharacteristically hot since last night. Even since building a nest, a warning bell has been ringing in her mind.

But Doctor Porter doesn't know any of that, so he just smiles. "I can get you some coffee if you'd like."

She shakes her head. "That's alright. I'm ready to speak with Erik."

"Perfect! Gerard will take you down to my office. I have a meeting in the Beta ward."

The Beta ward. Where she should have been in the first place if fate had been kinder to her.

"Sounds good," she says. "I'll see you at lunch."

The doctor waves, then disappears beyond another set of double doors.

She hears a grunt behind her, and Gerard walks past her, motioning for her to follow.

"Don't lock me in this time," she hisses, racing to catch up with him. "I mean it," she adds. "It could be dangerous."

He doesn't reply as they walk down the hallway.

"Why don't you like me?" she finally asks, as they reach the office door. "I know we got off to a poor start, but—"

"I have no reason *to* like you." He stuns her into silence as he opens the door.

She doesn't have time to process his words as Erik's scent

hits her like a freight train. Her eyes meet his dark ones, and his nostrils flare as stares at her. He keeps his face neutral, but she catches the tiniest bit of an eye twitch as she sits at the desk.

"Thank you," she says softly to Gerard, who turns away and shuts the door, leaving the two of them alone. Her body screams to run to him, to place herself in his lap and straddle him. His eyes burn into hers as he inhales, then they narrow.

"You smell like him," he barks out, and the spell is broken.

"I'm sorry?" she says, confused.

"You smell like Gerard."

His tone is dark and accusatory and laced with danger. Her mouth falls open in shock at the insinuation.

"He gave me a ride," she says slowly. "Because my car broke down. So yes, if you're saying I smell like cigarettes and sweat, I would agree with you."

His eyes soften. "Your car broke down?"

"Yes," she sighs. "Well, not broke down. The battery somehow died, or the car short-circuited. I have no idea, frankly."

He nods. "So, Gerard's been driving you?"

The accusatory tone is back, and she has to remind herself of the situation—she doesn't owe him an explanation. "Not that it's any of your business, but yes. He can't stand me if that makes you feel any better."

His full lips form into a thin line and he remains silent.

"We're not here to talk about that," she adds, keeping her tone professional. But she can practically feel the jealousy vibrating off him, and even his smell is darker with possession.

"You do a great job of that, you know," he replies, and she frowns.

"A great job of what?"

He nods towards the notepad in her lap. "Acting like

everything is normal. You have an exceptional talent for hiding your emotions when you want to."

Her face flames with embarrassment as she looks down at her notes. "I spoke to Doctor Porter about your issue with the suppressants," she says, and he raises an eyebrow.

"Oh, really?" he says as he gives her a smirk. "Changing the subject so suddenly?"

She refuses to take the bait. "He says it's so you don't go through any...*complications* if something happens."

His eyes are darker than she's ever seen them, and she shrinks back in her chair. Despite his relaxed form on the couch, she knows he could overpower her in one stride.

"Complications, Ellie? As if I went into a Rut, and there wasn't an Omega to satisfy me?"

They're playing a game she's not going to win.

He already won the moment she came apart on the phone with him, her fingers buried within herself.

He won the moment she returned the second time to see him.

Maybe he won before that when he got under her skin by taunting her.

"Right," she says, never breaking eye contact. "So, you don't suffer without an Omega."

"Good thing I have mine."

He stares her down, challenging her to disagree.

But she has to, because what he's saying is absurd.

"I'm not your Omega," she whispers. Yet, despite her mind screaming to *run,* she stays frozen in place.

"Like hell you aren't." He sits up slowly, leaning forward. "Don't deny what this is."

There's not enough air in the room. She looks back to the small window in the door, and fear races through her as she realizes Gerard is gone.

Again.

"You're right," he murmurs, following her gaze. "He

doesn't like you. If he cared at all, he wouldn't leave you alone with me."

"Don't." She whispers, a pathetic sound, and his eyes smolder.

Run. Run. Run.

Don't leave Alpha! We need Alpha!

There's a war in her mind, and she closes her eyes, trying to find her last shreds of reason.

But he smells so *good*, and if she could just stay here and talk to him...

"Stay with me," he whispers, and a familiar tingle races up her spine.

He's using Alpha Influence. She's only heard about it, but now she's hypnotized, her body easily obeying his will.

"Good girl," he praises, staying in his sitting position. "Now, we're going to talk, *really* talk. Do you understand?"

She's under his spell, the desire to obey him painful.

"Yes."

She'll talk. She'll tell him whatever he wants.

"I want to know everything about you, baby," he murmurs, and her heart stutters. "You tell me your secrets, and I'll tell you mine."

Fight it! Her mind screams.

But his scent envelopes her, giving her a familiar comfort, better than any nest could give her.

"Lock the door and move closer to me, Omega."

She shakes as she stands up, flipping the lock and trapping herself in the office with him.

Danger!

But Omega Ellie is more than happy to obey, moving the chair closer to the handsome, dangerous Alpha.

They're inches apart. Up close, she can see his faint stubble, a dark shadow on his pale skin. His eyes meet hers, and she drowns in his fiery gaze.

"Look at you," he whispers. "So beautiful. And all mine. Isn't that right, Omega?"

Somewhere in the back of her mind, she knows what he's doing is immoral.

But he's right, isn't he? Her body screams for him, her heart aches for him...

And she wants him to know her.

So she nods, and he gives her a small, genuine smile, his eyes crinkling in the corners.

It's beautiful.

He's so close to her he could reach out and touch her. His massive hands could wrap around her waist and position her on his lap, where she could straddle him and sink down on his cock...

But he keeps his hands to himself and asks a question that snaps her back to reality.

"Why were you so scared when the alarm went off?"

CHAPTER 14

ERIK

WHAT HE'S DONE IS UNFORGIVABLE.

Gerard *really* doesn't like her, though—he merely suggested he look the other way while he's in the office with Ellie, and the guard laughed and walked away as soon as he shut the door.

He'll have to do something about him later.

He doesn't know how long he has before Ellie leaves Green Woods forever—and he has to have a plan before that happens.

Part of that plan is uncovering her secrets.

"Why were you so scared when the alarm went off?"

As soon as he says it, he knows he went too far.

She snaps out of her stupor and gasps as the realization hits her. She glares at him with a look of horror and betrayal, her features eventually fading to sadness.

But she doesn't stand up and leave, nor does she yell at him.

Instead, she sighs, then looks back at him, resigned.

"I was in a car accident," she says quietly. "The car caught on fire after it flipped. I barely made it out."

The thought of her in danger makes his blood boil. "Fuck," he mutters. "That's horrible."

Her scent softens with a muted sadness, and she nods. "Yes. It was." To his surprise, she chuckles, looking down at her lap. "I never found the asshole that hit us. He just slammed into us, then drove off."

There's more to her story, he can tell by the look on her face.

"Us?"

She cringes. "My mother and sister."

He doesn't ask what happened, because he already knows.

They didn't make it out.

Her scent is tinged with the sourness of sorrow and grief. Guilt cuts through his hardened heart like a knife.

"I wish I could find him for you," he says. "I'd kill him."

She barks out a laugh as she stands up, moving her chair back to the desk. "Right. Me too."

And suddenly it clicks.

He recalls her words from the other day when he admitted to her that the murders were not random but were for revenge.

I understand, she had said, even though he could tell she instantly regretted her admission.

"I've tried, you know," she continues, her voice small, barely above a whisper. "I've tried to find him. There were witnesses, but the police didn't have enough to go on. They only had the type of truck, but nothing else."

She takes a long pause, and he sits and absorbs her words.

Her scent has changed again. Underneath the sweetness, there's a shame that floods her.

"You have survivor's guilt," he says, and she gives him a sad smile, one that doesn't reach her eyes.

She looks so *tired.*

"I was the reason we were in the car, Erik. I had just presented as an Omega and we were on our way back from my doctor's appointment."

He puts the pieces together in his mind, recalling their first encounter.

"That's why you hate being called an Omega. It reminds you of why they were in the car." He pauses, and she looks up at him again, her eyes shining. "You think it's your fault."

She clears her throat and looks away from him; her gaze finding the window, staring out into the trees. They sit there in silence, and his heart aches for her.

He wants to tell her it's not her fault, that she's a fucking angel, and too good for this world.

He wants to promise her he'll avenge her and her family, and she'll never have to suffer again.

He'll burn the fucking world down for her if only he could tear her grief from her soul.

But he merely watches her observing as the light illuminates her face, taking in her beauty and sorrow.

The clock ticks behind them, the minutes going by, both of them sitting in silence, their scents entwining.

It's just enough to be around her, he decides.

"Why did you turn yourself in?" she asks, still looking out the window.

The question catches him off guard. "You've been researching me, Miss Winters?"

A corner of her lip turns up. "Of course. You had no reason to turn yourself in. You weren't even a *suspect*." She swivels the chair back to face him. "So, why? You want to be here for the rest of your life?"

He stays silent, and she grows angry.

"You could at least tell me that, after you intruded on my private thoughts," she snaps. "After you had the gall to demand to know my secrets."

He knows she's right, and her anger is so beautiful, so sexy, that he just...

"They had someone else," he says simply. "They arrested an innocent man. I turned myself in so he wouldn't spend a lifetime behind bars."

Her eyes widen, then she chuckles, shaking her head. "Wow. Your moral compass is something else."

"I could say the same for you, baby," he says, a smirk forming on his face. "Such a professional during the day, yet you spread your legs for me at night."

Her face flames. "Yes, and it was a mistake," she snaps. "Something that won't happen again."

He grins. "I heard those words last time," he says. "I don't think it will be the last time I hear them, either."

She scowls, but he can smell the arousal on her, the scent speaking directly to his cock.

But his victory is short-lived as she glances at the clock and stands up from her chair. "We're done for the day," she says. "I need to meet with Doctor Porter. Do you want me to relay any message from you?"

"Yes. Tell him I require around-the-clock behavioral analysis, or else we won't make progress."

She glares at him. "You're a psychopath."

He barks out a laugh. "You already knew that, baby. But I thought you weren't supposed to use such harsh judgments on your clients?"

She huffs then stops at the door, her hand on the lock.

"And Erik," she says, giving him one last look, "use Influence on me again, and I'll fucking kill you."

He doesn't stop laughing as she leaves.

CHAPTER 15

ELLIE

SHE'S DONE.

She hurries down the hallway, frustrated that there's no sign of Gerard.

Erik used his Influence on her, *again*, and coerced her out of her own secrets. She was ready to open up to him, to let him do whatever he wanted to her.

Fuck *that*.

Her secrets are her own, her story belongs to *her*. It wasn't his to know.

She shouldn't work with him anymore; much less be in the same town as him.

And she can't even *leave* Green Woods, because rain and hail trap the town in a cage of cold.

Even if her car was working, she couldn't drive in the weather.

Doctor Porter is in the lobby, and he frowns when he sees her face.

"Are you alright, Miss Winters?" he asks, as Gerard comes into view. He meets her eye, and she takes a deep breath.

"No. Gerard needs to be outside the door at all times. It's unacceptable that he wasn't."

The guard is livid, almost snarling at her when Doctor Porter turns to him. "Were you not guarding the door, Gerard?"

But his face smooths out when he regards the doctor. "I used the restroom for a moment, sir. My apologies, Miss Winters," he says, turning to face her.

His eyes scream of death, but her rage matches his.

Doctor Porter seems to notice, and he clears his throat awkwardly. "Actually, I would like to have a meeting with you later in my office. I can give you a ride home if you'd like."

His kindness warms her heart, and her rage quiets. "Yes," she says. "I would like that very much."

"Alright. I'll be in the Beta ward for now, but feel free to continue to use my office in the meantime."

She doesn't want to. Erik's scent will still be in the air, and she'll have to fight every instinct to roll around on the couch like an animal.

But, it's that or staying in the lobby with Gerard, who looks at her like she's the scum of the earth.

She chooses the office.

HER REPORTS TO LITA ARE A JOKE.

Instead of learning more about Alpha behaviors and how they're affected by confinement and the prison system, she's only learning about Erik.

It's the exact opposite of what she went here to do.

So, she fills her reports with false observations and conclusions.

Every time she's alone with him, their conversation steers to something...not productive.

How *dare* he.

She fumes silently at his invasive behavior, abusing his Alpha Influence to turn her into a submissive Omega, ready to satisfy his every desire.

And the worst part is she had no idea Alpha Influence was real.

It had never happened to her before, or to any of her Omega friends. It was only whispered about, along with rumors that only the strongest Alphas could perform it.

And they could only do it to their mates.

Shit.

An uncomfortable hope swells in her chest, and she hates herself even more as she sends an email that inaccurately reflects her time at Green Woods.

It's only been a week, but it feels like a fucking year.

Doctor Porter enters the office, and she quickly rushes out of her chair and moves to the couch. She catches a whiff of *Erik,* and she tries to calm her rapidly beating heart.

He closes the door behind him, then sits and sighs. "Ellie, I'm so sorry about Gerard. He should have guarded the door at all times."

She thinks back to Gerard's snarling face and backtracks. "It's fine, really."

"He didn't..." The doctor struggles as if trying to find the correct words. "Were you..."

This is her chance.

She could tell Doctor Porter everything.

The phone. The Influence. The remarks Gerard made to her.

She would never have to see Erik again.

It's the right thing to do.

But she shakes her head and smiles. "Erik has been perfect. But I would love to still compare notes, as well."

She threw her chance out the window.

"Of course," he says. "Speaking of, I wanted to ask if you'd like another project. I know it's only been a week, but what do you think about working with some of our Betas as well?"

The question catches her off guard. "Really?" she asks, surprised.

"Yes. If Erik took a liking to you, I don't doubt you'll do great with a few of our other inmates. Especially because that's what you came here for in the first place. And the more research, the better, right?"

She's stunned at his request. Her eyes light up and she gives him a genuine smile. "Yes! Absolutely. Thank you so much."

This is her opportunity to stay away from Erik and get back in touch with reality.

The doctor grins back at her. "This is perfect. It's so refreshing to have someone around that actually *cares* about our people. We haven't had someone like you in a long time."

His words confuse her. "I understand Erik is a difficult client, but why have you had trouble finding more people?" She asks.

"Ah. Well, location for one. We're not exactly a tourist attraction. But also..." The doctor looks away, his brow furrowed. "I'm not sure if I should tell you this."

She freezes in her chair, fear creeping up her spine.

It has to do with Erik. She just *knows* it does.

"All of them have quit after their first session with Erik."

It makes sense, of course.

He's a monster and master manipulator. Anyone with half a shred of sanity would run screaming when they meet him.

Just like she should have.

But she keeps her face carefully neutral as she speaks. "Well, I'm still here. So, maybe that tells you something."

"Yes. Maybe he's changing," he says wistfully. "Anyway, I

would love to start you next week with a Beta inmate. I think you two will work well together."

Yes, anything to be distracted, she thinks desperately. She needs anything at all to keep Erik from her traitorous Omega heart.

CHAPTER 16

ELLIE

SHE SPENDS SATURDAY PURGING ERIK FROM HER MIND.

Or at least, she tries.

She purposely looks at the crime scene photos once again, keeping the pictures open on her laptop screen and burning his cruelty into her mind.

When that doesn't work, she does more research on him. His net worth is astronomical, a sum so large that he could buy Green Woods if he wanted to.

Again, she stares at his picture, trying to understand the man who would talk an inmate into taking their own life, yet turn themselves in because an innocent man would go to prison in his place.

Then, she looks up his sister.

Cassandra Hart was ten years his junior, dying at twenty years old.

Juliet's age.

Images of her own sister flash in her mind, and she blinks

back tears. If she thinks about her too long, she'll drown in a sea of guilt.

Despite everything, her heart aches for Erik as she reads about his sister.

She finds a picture of them together at an event, his arm casually slung around her shoulders. He's carefree and joyful. His dark eyes are gentle, with no trace of malice.

Of course, cyber stalking him isn't helping her situation.

She needs to relax and double her dose of suppressants.

As if on cue, a violent cramp hits her.

"Fuck," she hisses, clutching her stomach and doubling over onto the bed. A gush of slick dampens her underwear as she limps to the bathroom, washing herself up.

She hasn't had a Heat in over a year because of her suppressants. She hoped the makeshift nest and the slick were due to her attraction to Erik and nothing more.

But her fevered skin and painful nipples say otherwise.

This is bad.

Very bad.

Another cramp hits her womb.

"Oh God," she gasps as she strips off her clothes, hobbling back to the bed. Naked and under the sheets, she wraps herself in blankets and wills her body to relax.

But it won't. Her traitorous mind fills yet again with thoughts of *him,* and how desperate she is to be touched and loved.

It's pathetic, really, if she thinks about it. But no amount of shaming herself stops her body from crying out for him.

Her phone buzzes, and it's from the unknown number again.

Working with other people now? I'm not sure I'll allow that to happen. I want you to myself, baby.

She bites her lip and groans, shifting under the covers.

"Please kick in, *please,*" she begs the suppressants, hoping somehow they'll listen to her.

She keeps her eyes closed, pulls the blankets up to her chest, and eventually dozes off.

———

SHE KNOWS THIS ROAD.

Mom took the back way from the hospital, trying to get them home faster.

"It's going to be fine, Ellie," Juliet says from the front passenger seat. "They sent you home with tons of painkillers. The first Heat is always the worst, anyway."

She can only reply with a groan, partly from the cramps, and partly from never wanting to discuss a Heat with her sister.

They're nearing a quiet road with two thin lanes. Far off in the distance, a vehicle approaches, going the opposite way.

It's the red truck.

"Mom, pull over!" she tries to scream, but her lips stay shut, only a muffled sound escaping.

The truck comes closer.

She tries to memorize the license plate, but the numbers and letters are a blur.

"PULL OVER!"

She thrashes around in the backseat, begging them to listen to her, and don't they see how the truck is swerving—

BOOM.

SHE WAKES GASPING AND SHIVERING, THE COLD AIR hurting her throat.

The room is pitch back and *freezing.*

Thunder roars overhead, and the wind howls, the violent storm causing the walls to shake.

Frantically, she rolls out of bed and tries the light switch near the door. When that doesn't work, she attempts to turn on the bathroom lights, to no avail.

88

Oh no.

The power's out.

Judging by how cold the cabin is, it's probably been out for a while.

She grabs her phone and deletes every text and missed call from Erik. Then she checks the weather for Green Woods, tears of frustration filling her eyes as she sees the temperature.

She won't make it through the night if the power doesn't come back on.

Her phone buzzes with an incoming call, and she answers it immediately.

"Doctor Porter?" she breathes, her voice thick with emotion.

"Ellie! Are you alright? Do you still have electricity?"

Tears of frustration spill down her cheeks. "No, I don't."

"Oh, no, that's not good," he murmurs. "My home is out as well. Unfortunately, it looks like you and I will have to stay at the facility tonight, as they have backup generators."

NO. NO. NO.

"I...would that be appropriate, do you think?" Her voice shakes as she tries to argue with him.

"Not really, but we don't have a choice, do we?"

I do. I could freeze here tonight, just so I don't throw myself at your favorite prisoner.

"I think I'll be able to ride it out."

The doctor laughs. "Absolutely not. I'll be picking you up as soon as possible. We have a hospital wing with beds. You'll have a set of keys as well. It's only temporary, most likely just for tonight."

Oh, God.

She's going to be in the same building as Erik for the night.

"Alright," she says weakly. "I'll pack a bag."

CHAPTER 17

ERIK

SHE'S GOING TO BE WORKING WITH ANOTHER PATIENT.

A *Beta*.

Doctor Porter mentioned it proudly, with his excitement for his new pupil outweighing the rationale of not sharing private information with Erik.

It should be fine, really. Yet, he's not sure how he feels about his darling Omega being in the same room as another mass murderer.

Him being the exception, of course.

He wants all her time to be spent with him. No one else should talk to her, let alone look at her.

She's too precious for this world, let alone any of the cretins she wants to help.

Fuck.

And now, she has the audacity to ignore his texts, even though she won't be in the building all weekend.

He'll punish her for it later.

But for now, he needs to do more research.

It only takes a few minutes to find the death certificates of Ellie's mother and sister, and his heart aches for his Omega.

He thinks about the smiles she fakes so easily and her talent for hiding any negative emotions from her face.

No one should need that ability.

He could sense her guilt when she spoke of the car accident, and it was like looking in a mirror. They're more alike than she realizes, and the selfish part of him rejoices.

If he bares his soul to her, lays down his heart at her feet, perhaps she would understand.

He plans to tell her, eventually.

If the time comes.

———

THE LIGHTS DIM AND HE HEARS THE GENERATORS click on.

It's not the first time they've had an outage, but this storm is particularly violent with the wind shaking the windows and the thunder raging outside.

He thinks of her and worries. He can't imagine the tiny cabin is well-equipped to deal with this kind of weather.

Are you alright?

He sends the message, hoping she'll respond, trying to calm the panic that rises in his chest.

She's from Los Angeles. She's not used to this type of weather.

Message not delivered.

Maybe Gerard gave her a ride out of town before the storm hit.

Maybe she quit.

That's going to make his plan a lot more difficult.

The door to his cell unlocks and Gerard enters, his eyes shooting to the phone in Erik's hand.

The Alpha raises an eyebrow, challenging him to say

anything about the contraband. Of course, the Beta doesn't comment on it.

"Doctor Porter will be here during the storm," he says, looking anywhere but at Erik. "He's looking to have an extra session with you this weekend."

But he barely registers the doctor's words, as Ellie's Omega scent hits him.

A low rumble builds in his chest as he narrows his eyes at Gerard. "*She's* here," he rumbles. "Isn't she?"

But he already knows the answer. He smells her lust and desperation.

Her Heat is coming soon.

"She is," Gerard confirms.

"Where is she staying?"

It's not a question, it's a demand.

"I'm not sure. Wherever Doctor Porter puts her."

It's no matter. He'll find her.

He motions toward the guard's key. "How much?"

Gerard's eyes widen. "For my *keys?*"

"I know you have an extra set. Name your price."

"You're out of your fucking mind if you think—"

"Fifty thousand," he interrupts. It's a cheap offer, but Gerard doesn't know it. He'd pay ten million if he needed to, just to have a set of keys.

The guard's eyes are wide, his mouth hanging open in disbelief. "How—"

"I'll send it to you right now, electronically." Erik holds up the phone. "From my bank."

Gerard sputters, shaking his head. "Bullshit. There's no way—"

"Keep talking, and I lower it to ten thousand."

The Beta quickly spews out his banking information, and within seconds, Gerard is fifty thousand dollars richer.

"It would help if you left for the night, too," Erik adds nonchalantly.

"Are you going to kill her?" Gerard asks quietly.

The Alpha snarls at him. "Do you think I'd fucking kill an Omega? Give me your keys before I take them myself."

Spooked, Gerard tosses his set of keys, leaving the cell door open. "Porter's in his office right now," he says quickly. "Just make sure he doesn't catch you."

"And Gerard?" Erik says, just as the guard turns to leave. "I won't forget how easily you put Ellie at risk."

The Beta pales and hurries off.

Erik stands up and shuts the cell door, preparing himself for what's coming.

CHAPTER 18

ELLIE

SHE CAN SMELL HIM AS SOON AS THEY STEP INSIDE THE building.

He's *irresistible.*

She could cry at how welcoming it is to know she's near him.

She screams internally.

He's killed people, Ellie.

He's not a good man.

She's lost in her panic as Doctor Porter shows her the hospital wing, leading her to her room.

"It's not the most comfortable," the doctor says. "But there are extra blankets in the drawers, and it locks from the inside. Only Gerard has a key."

Blankets. Build a nest.

"Thank you," she whispers, clutching her duffel bag to her chest.

"Is there anything you need? I'll camp in my office tonight, so I won't be far."

She swallows and hesitates. "If you have any fever reducer, that would be great. And any extra...suppressants."

It shouldn't be a bad word, but it is. To her, it's embarrassing, and another reason why she shouldn't work with Doctor Porter.

It's a reminder that she's the reason her family is gone.

But Doctor Porter is unphased at her request. "I'm sure we have some somewhere," he says. "I would run to the drugstore for you if this damn storm wasn't so reckless."

True to his word, he returns in under a minute, handing Ellie a handful of pills and a water bottle. "Will this work?"

She takes two generic brand suppressants immediately, swallowing them down as the doctor watches.

"Yes," she says, giving him her best fake smile. "Thank you."

"I'm going to retire for the night," he says, smiling back. "Gerard's here, I'm here, and then we only have the one Alpha and Beta inmate. You're completely safe."

No, I'm not, she thinks. *He knows I'm here. He'll find me.*

But she tells the doctor goodnight, and he leaves her alone in the room with the dull hum of the generators to keep her company.

She sets up as many blankets as she can to make the bed more comfortable. There's a small bathroom in the corner, and she brushes her teeth and tries to ready herself for bed.

The door is locked. She made sure of it.

Her skin is still overheated despite the chill in the room. The slick has stopped for the moment, but she's horrified it will leak again and Erik will smell it.

She needs to sleep.

Wrapping herself in as many blankets as she can, she settles into the bed, using the remote to adjust it to her comfort. She keeps the overhead light on, not ready to surrender to the darkness.

She finally checks her phone after putting it off for so long.

There's one missed call from Lita, and one new text from Erik.

Are you alright?

It's stupid, really, how her heart swells at the message.

Alpha cares for us!

But the joy is short-lived as she reminds herself of who he is.

No matter how badly she may want him, he's off limits.

None of this is fair.

He's the first person who won't judge her for the hatred of herself and for the person who was driving the truck.

He wouldn't judge her for her sick need for revenge, or the daydreams of torturing the man to death.

The one person who could truly understand her is sentenced to life in an institution.

So, she allows herself the tears, gently crying herself to sleep, hoping that the suppressants will do their job and postpone her Heat over for a few more days.

It's freezing.

Even under the blankets, the chilly air stings her lungs, and she curls into a ball, shivering.

She groans, opening her eyes, but sees nothing but darkness.

The light isn't on, and the hum of the generators has stopped.

It's *too* cold.

"Oh no," she breathes, sitting up in bed, feeling around for anything with a power source.

But the air physically hurts, and she wraps herself back in the blankets, unable to leave the bed.

The power's out.

The wind howls, and she presses her body deeper into the mattress.

Cold. I'm so cold.

Her teeth chatter and her breath comes out in quick puffs, goosebumps rising on every inch of her body.

How ironic, she thinks, *that I'll die freezing to death, while my family burned to death.*

The lock to her door rattles, and she prays it's the wind playing tricks on her.

It has to be the wind. He can't get in here.

The door *creaks* open, and she keeps as still as possible.

If I hide under the blankets, the monster won't get me.

The scent of pepper and citrus caresses her as her heart races.

He's only a breath away, and then his weight is covering her.

She kicks out and tries to scream, but his massive hand covers her mouth.

"Shh, shh, baby, it's me," he whispers in her ear. She shakes as he curls around her, a heavy weight in the dark.

"You're so cold," he murmurs, and she whimpers. "You're too cold. That's not good, sweetheart."

He removes his hand from her mouth and pulls her close to him, wrapping his arms around her. It's the most comfort she's felt in ages.

She forgot what it's like to be held.

"Go-go-away," she breathes, her voice barely a whisper. "You sh-shouldn't b-be here."

"You're freezing," he hushes her, his hand smoothing away the hair from her neck. He places a gentle kiss there, his lips soft and warm, and she fights back a moan. "It's too cold out here. It's dangerous, sweetheart. You never know what monsters roam in the shadows."

"N-no," she hisses, even as she instinctively snuggles up

against him, her back soaking up the warmth from his chest. "I don't want you."

He hums. "I think you're a little liar, Omega."

She doesn't know how he fits in the tiny bed, but she's thankful all the same. With her ass to him, she can feel his massive cock pushing against her. His scent caresses her, sending waves of pleasure throughout her body.

It's wrong, for so many reasons.

"H-how did you get in?" she whispers, and his mouth finds her again, this time at the juncture of her shoulder and neck. His tongue finds her gland, flicking it gently back and forth, and she arches her back against him.

"I have my ways," he murmurs, his voice low and silky. "You should know by now I can do anything."

They're still separated by blankets, but his body warmth is enough to take away the chill, and she allows him to continue his assault on her neck, his lips and tongue working gently on her skin. Slick drips out of her, soaking through her panties as her pussy clenches.

He's going to make her come just from his gentle touches.

"Just feel," he whispers. "Don't think."

And she doesn't. In complete darkness, she can't see anything, but she can *feel*. Her hand reaches out behind her to touch his hair, the locks thick and soft. He groans as she pulls it and she moans at the sounds he makes.

The storm rages outside, the wind howling, drowning out her gasps and soft cries. His body engulfs her, his hand dipping lower, ghosting over her nipples. He plays with one gently, rubbing over the blankets, until he pinches hard.

"Fuck," she moans, and he hisses in response.

"You know what I wanted to do the first time I saw you?" he whispers, and she shakes her head as he continues his fondling. "I wanted to fucking devour you. Make you forget everything except the way my hands, mouth, and cock feel on you."

"Oh..." She grinds her ass hard against his cock, their bodies still separated by the blankets wrapped around her. Her back arches and she's almost over the edge, just from him touching her.

"I wanted to pump you full of my cum until you couldn't move. Make you my good little slut."

That does it. She lets out a hoarse scream, grinding shamelessly against him as she soaks herself with slick, her body convulsing.

"Oh, fuck," he groans. "Keep coming, baby. Good girl, soaking yourself for me."

He sucks on her gland, *hard*, and a second wave hits her. He knows exactly how to touch her, and he plays her body perfectly, making her beg for more.

Then, he maneuvers her, turning her around, so she's facing him. In the dark, she can't see his face, but she reaches out, running her hand over rough stubble. She finds his lips, then leans in and kisses him, desperate for more contact.

It takes him by surprise. She leans her body against him, tugging at his hair as she presses her lips against him, and he freezes in shock. But he quickly regains his composure and plunges his tongue into her mouth, growling.

He tastes of spice and mint, and she can't help but moan as he devours her.

"Touch me," she begs, pulling away from his mouth to gasp for air. "Please."

His clever hands find their way to the blankets, pulling them down as she kicks them off, leaving her in only her tank top and sweats. The air is still painfully cold, but his body heat acts as the perfect furnace, with his mouth placing searing kisses down her flesh.

She wastes no time in pulling her tank top off, exposing her breasts to him.

"Fuck," he hisses, his hand traveling down her chest. "I wish I could see you right now."

His fingers find her nipple as the other hand gently cups the back of her head, keeping her in place as he teases her with his fingers.

"How...how do you know how to touch me like this?" she gasps, arching her back. "I've never...I haven't..."

It's never been like this. With anyone.

"Because we're mates," he whispers, his mouth traveling to her collarbone. "Because you're *mine*."

Warning bells ring in the back of her mind, but she doesn't have time to argue as his wet mouth sucks on her nipple painfully hard, teasing the peak with his tongue. He switches his attention to the other one, and she grips his hair and pulls as he tongues her body ruthlessly.

Her sweats are the next to come off, but he makes no move to help her as she undresses, instead keeping his attention on her chest.

He's letting her be in control. She's giving, and he's taking.

"Erik," she gasps, and he growls into her chest. "Please. More."

Suddenly, he removes his mouth from her chest, and she cries out as the cold air hits her. His weight leaves the bed, and she wants to scream in frustration. She's terrified he's leaving, abandoning her to her loneliness and arousal, but large hands pull her ankles, positioning her so her ass is flat against the bed, her legs spread obscenely.

Lightning flashes.

It lights up the room for a moment, and she sees the Alpha standing over the bed, his enormous frame towering over her. His face is dark, his expression one of desperation and hunger.

Her fear spikes, and she knows he can smell it.

"You only want me to fuck you in the dark, baby?" he asks, as her vision fades. "You want your monster only when you don't have to look at him?"

She bites her lip and whimpers.

She hears rustling, then his breath ghosts across her cunt. "Lucky for you," he murmurs. "I don't mind."

Then his mouth is on her, and she can't contain her screams.

CHAPTER 19

ERIK

HE'S THE LUCKIEST BASTARD IN THE WORLD.

He expected her to scream and put up a fight and maybe kick him in the balls.

He never dreamed his mouth would be where it is right now, her willingly grinding her pussy on his face, begging him to make her come.

Her slick stains his face and drips down his cheeks and chin obscenely as he eats her out. He sucks on her clit as if it's the last time he'll be able to.

But it can't be. It just *can't*.

He had an outline of a plan, before. But now that he's tasted her...

There's no way he will ever let her go.

He murmurs it into her pussy and she moans so loudly the thunder barely muffles the noise. Her thighs clamp around his face, squeezing tightly, but he would happily die buried in her honeyed slick.

One finger barely fits inside her, and his dick throbs

painfully against his pants as he stretches her out. She stops breathing when he inserts the second one, her cunt contracting around him, and he groans.

"You're so *tight*," he hisses against her thigh. "How are you ever going to take my knot, baby? I'll split you open."

He presses a kiss to her clit, lazily sucking, and she explodes.

She's babbling now, her words a combination of *please-Erikyesplease* as she rides out her orgasm, convulsing on the bed. As she comes down from the high, he strokes her clit lazily, his tongue lapping up as much of her delicious juices as he can.

His cock is so hard he might explode.

He removes his fingers from her and brings them to his lips, sucking them clean, his eyes rolling into the back of his head at her taste.

Fuck.

She whimpers as he feels his way towards the bed, climbing in to join her.

"Baby." He presses a kiss to her lips as she hums.

"Hmm?"

"Are you going into Heat tonight?"

She pauses.

If I took you tonight, could you handle me leaving before the sun comes up?

If she's going into Heat, he won't be able to knot her. He needs to leave her in a few hours, and he can't do that if he's locked inside her cunt.

"I—I took suppressants," she breathes. "Before I went to bed."

He chuckles. *Of course she did.* "And you thought that would keep me away, sweetheart?"

She shifts uncomfortably, but he holds her still, cradling her face in his hands. "You and I both know," he purrs, "that suppressants only stop the Heat. Not the attraction."

She tries to squirm away, but he holds her steady, swinging a thigh over hers. "You're not going to deny this, *us*, anymore, are you, Ellie?"

Her scent spikes at his words, and she groans. "Not tonight, no," she whispers.

He scoffs. "Not tonight," he whispers. "But in the morning, you will. My sweet Omega. You're always so good at lying to herself."

He's startled, but not surprised, as she lands a slap across his cheek.

"Fuck you," she hisses, struggling in his grip.

"That's the plan," he growls as her scent grows sweeter. "But only if you're a good girl."

Another slap, and he's able to grab her hands and pin them over her head.

It's an incredible skill in the dark, really. She should be impressed.

But she's as stubborn as ever, now that she's gotten off.

"You're a bastard," she hisses, even as she lifts her lips, grinding against his clothed erection. Her slick stains the front of his pants, and he groans.

"I am," he agrees. "The worst kind of monster. But you seem to like it."

She arches her back, her wet pussy spreading slick all over the front of him. "I don't like anything about you," she gasps, her tone far from convincing.

"I can name some things you like about me," he whispers back, his mouth descending to her neck. He presses gentle kisses against her soft skin, and soon she's mewling, grinding against him recklessly.

"Fuck," he groans. "You're soaking us both, baby."

The lightning flashes, and he glimpses her perfect body in the light, the opening of her cunt glistening with slick. Her eyes match the hunger in his, with her delicate mouth slightly parted in anticipation. She struggles against his grip, and he lets one of her hands go free as she reaches for his cock, squeezing *hard*.

The room grows dark again.

He moans deeply, and she grips harder.

"Oh, fuck," she whispers. "You're so *big*. I've never..."

And he realizes with a triumph that she's never been with another Alpha.

"*Mine*," he growls, as he lets her other hand go free. She sits up and reaches for him, pulling him in for another kiss, her tongue licking her juices from his mouth.

His girl is positively filthy.

Her hands tug at his shirt, and he pulls it off, tossing it to the floor. Cold fingers run up and down his chest, feeling every muscle that was hiding underneath the cotton scrubs.

She doesn't see the smirk on his face as she hums in approval at his sculpted body.

But suddenly she takes control, pushing him back on the bed and straddling him. His hands find her hips and grip tightly, as his Omega takes what she wants.

CHAPTER 20

ELLIE

She's a feral, wild thing.

Maybe it's the storm, disguising her sins as she takes her pleasure from the inmate.

Her inmate.

She's a woman possessed, allowing her baser instincts to take control as she explores his body.

His scent fuels her, with his mix of pepper and citrus speaking directly to her cunt. Her body burns as she straddles him, grinding herself against his erection.

She's torturing him, and she loves it. His cock is rock hard under his pants as she drags her cunt up and down his throbbing dick.

That's what he gets for being an obsessive son of a bitch.

That's what he gets for torturing her with text messages and making her come apart on the phone just from the sound of his fucking *voice*.

This is his punishment for using his Influence and forcing her to reveal the secrets she tries to bury.

This is his punishment for ruining her fucking life.

Maybe she speaks the last part out loud, because he grips her hips so painfully she knows they'll bruise.

"Punish me, then," he hisses. "Make me pay, *Omega*."

She moves off him for a moment, tugging down his pants to touch him.

Oh.

He's warm steel in her grip, her hand unable to fit around his width. She swipes the tip with her thumb and he jolts, gasping at her touch.

Yes. She could get used to this.

Sitting over him, she works him slowly, allowing her fist to run up and down his length, gripping his massive cock tightly.

"Fuck," he hisses, "Ellie——"

She can't wait any longer. Straddling him, she works his tip inside her, then sinks down on him slowly.

"Oh," she gasps, moving as gently as she can to accommodate his girth. She's soaked, her slick acting as a perfect lubrication as she finally sinks all the way down, his cock twitching inside her.

Her cunt grips him, and he groans.

She could come just like this, squeezing his length with her inner walls, but she knows there are much better ways to bring release.

She slowly moves her hips, working his cock inside her.

It's *perfect*.

She's thankful that the storm blocks out her moans. She uses his cock, bouncing on him, taking what she needs, rubbing her clit furiously.

She uses him, and it feels incredible. He's groaning something, possibly her name, but she doesn't care. Her energy is focused on having the head of his cock hit a sensitive spot deep inside her.

But he's impatient, and he snaps his hips up, fucking up

into her. Her body shakes with the pressure, and she can't stop the screams that leave her mouth.

She's coming before she can warn him.

Her eyes roll into the back of her head, and she grows rigid, gripping his length so tightly he can barely continue to fuck her. She tries to say his name, but no words come out, only gasps of pleasure.

She's on her back before she can blink, him fucking her ruthlessly, pounding them both into the flimsy mattress as the bed creaks and shakes.

She loses track of how long she orgasms, but he gives her words of praise, murmuring depravities in her ear as she rides out her pleasure.

He takes his time with her, turning her over onto all fours so he can take her from behind, her mind a haze of lust and pleasure.

"Alpha," she moans out, and he stiffens inside her.

"Fuck, fuck," he chants. "Gonna knot you, Omega."

She's in a delirious state when she feels him inflate, his massive cock stuffing her walls, filling her in a way she didn't think possible.

Her voice is gone, and her legs are ready to give out. He empties his cum into her, roaring in time with the thunder outside.

She collapses against him, his cock still twitching inside her, as he rolls them on to their side.

She promptly passes out.

THE STORM RAGES ON.

She opens her eyes. The grey light of early morning begins to fill the room. His fingers lazily draw circles on her back, and she sighs against him, content. Sometime in the night he slipped out of her, and now they spoon with his arms wrapped tightly around her.

Her mind is quiet, and she's at peace.

At this moment, they could be anyone. They're just a man and a woman sharing an intimate night together.

He breaks the spell when he speaks, his mouth close to her ear.

"My younger sister was an Omega," he says softly. He continues to draw circles on her back, but she stiffens at his words. "She was beaten to death by three Alphas."

She stops breathing.

He takes in a breath. "She turned one of them down. He grabbed his friends, and they took turns with her until she died."

Tears prick at the corner of her eyes. "I'm sorry," she whispers. "I'm so sorry."

His fingers stop moving, and he pulls her closer to his chest. "She was my only family," he admits. "I killed all three of them." His voice is empty as he continues. "It took me a month of planning. I made them apologize and beg for mercy until I was tired of hearing them scream."

The tears spill down her cheeks, and her heart aches for him. "I know," she says. "I saw the pictures."

He sighs into her hair but remains silent.

"Did you...why didn't you tell them—" Her voice chokes on the words, and she can't finish her question.

"No one needs to know what happened to her. She doesn't deserve her memory tarnished in that way. I'd rather people remember her for who she was."

Her resolve crumbles and her heart breaks at his words. "I miss my sister, too. So much," she whispers. "No one deserves that kind of pain. There are days where I can't breathe from the sorrow of missing my mom and sister. I wouldn't wish it on anyone."

"If I could take your pain away, I would," he says softly.

"I wish I could do the same for you," she whispers.

He places a gentle kiss on the top of her head. "You can tell me about them, if you'd like," he says softly. "One day."

They remain silent until the sun creeps in.

She's not ready to look at him. The secrets they shared in the dark are too much to bear in the light.

"I have to go soon," he says, his voice wistful.

"I know," she murmurs.

He presses another kiss to the top of her head.

"Do you hate me?" he asks after a moment.

Do you hate me for what I've done to you? What I am?

"No. I could never hate you," she admits.

He huffs out a laugh and grips her tighter. "We'll see."

Before she can ask what he means, he slips out of bed. Her body is freezing without him, even as the whirr of the generators finally kicks on, heat blowing back into the room.

Lamplight fills the room, and she looks up at him, taking in the contours of his face. He's striking and intense, and in his own twisted way, handsome.

He's her dark knight, who won't save the day.

"Go back to sleep," he orders her, and it's easy to obey him. The door *clicks* behind him, and she falls into a dream-less sleep

CHAPTER 21

ERIK

HIS PLAN IS SOLIDIFYING.

Gerard shows up in the late morning to retrieve his keys.

"I'll wipe the security footage," Erik informs him, "so you can keep your job."

"You can do that?" the guard asks. "It's that easy?"

"I built half of these programs. It takes a few codes, and all the footage is lost from the last two days."

Gerard looks impressed, but weary. "Sounds good."

"I'll give you another fifty thousand for your second set of keys," Erik offers. "The ones in the front office."

Gerard's eyes practically bulge out of his head. "Done," he offers quickly. "And you'll make sure I won't get caught?"

Erik scoffs. "If they can't catch me, they won't catch you. Just get them to me as soon as possible."

"Damn," the guard sighs. "She's worth that much, huh? All for a piece of pussy?"

Erik advances on him is a second, his blood boiling with rage.

"She's...worth...*everything*," Erik snarls, backing him into the doorway. "And don't ever fucking talk about her like that again."

Gerard scurries out to retrieve the set of keys.

He *really* doesn't like Gerard. His attitude towards Ellie is unacceptable, and he's going to need to take action soon.

But that's secondary to his first plan; the one where he makes his girl his forever. Now that he's had a taste, it won't be enough.

She's the only one who can understand him. She's the only one that can look up at him with wonder and make him feel like he has a heart again.

But to make things easier, he needs access to Doctor Porter's office, and uninterrupted time with his computer.

And the sooner he can have it, the better.

———

"I need to ask you something."

Doctor Porter pulls him into his office at the end of the weekend.

Erik smiles to himself. Doctor Porter has been more open about Ellie than he realizes. He takes mental notes of every piece of information and files them away for future reference.

But, to his surprise, it's not about her.

"Have you noticed anything unusual about Gerard?" The doctor looks anywhere but at Erik, frowning.

Oh, this is *perfect*.

"How do you mean?" He does his best to sound ignorant.

"Have you seen any of his interactions with Ellie?" the doctor asks, his brow furrowed. "Does he make her uncomfortable?"

That gets his attention. "Has something happened?" He leans forward on the couch, a low growl forming in his throat.

"I can't prove it, but I believe he's been a bit inappropriate with her. If you see anything, please let me know."

He sees red. His fists clench, his nails digging into his palm.

He hurt Omega.

"Inappropriate with her *how?*" he hisses.

The doctor shrugs, frustrated. "Some comments, I believe. She won't clarify, but I would wager it has something to do with her Omega status."

He looks at Erik pointedly. "I know you think she's... special. And she's important to you."

Erik shrugs. "She's good at her job, and I'm not a fan of anyone who disrespects an Omega."

"Right. Well, if you see anything, let me know."

"I will."

They continue their session and Erik gives rehearsed answers, reciting the words he knows the doctor wants to hear.

But all he's focused on is Gerard.

He wonders if the guard knows how much time he has left.

CHAPTER 22

ELLIE

THE POWER IS BACK ON IN THE CABIN AND SHE TAKES Sunday to gather her senses.

Her Heat is still inevitable, an explosion that she knows will happen sooner rather than later.

She'll be able to take Heat leave, of course. She knows Doctor Porter would understand.

Her mind wanders, fueled by anxiety and distress.

What she did with Erik was...

Unforgivable.

Unacceptable.

And yet, her heart still aches for him, now that she understands the reasoning behind his crime.

Would she do the same if she had the chance? If she could take revenge on the driver that hit her family, would she do something awful as well?

She's not sure of the answer, and she spends the rest of the weekend gritting her teeth and fighting the nausea that threatens to overtake her.

To distract herself, she explores the dusty basement, taking note of the double locking mechanism from the inside. Besides an obscene amount of dust, she finds nothing of interest.

She wants to hide in the damn basement and die of shame.

There are missed calls from Lita, but she can't bring herself to call her back. She sends her a message instead.

I'm fine. Just busy. Will email you the reports next week.

And, of course, a text from Erik.

I'm never letting you go.

Her heart beats wildly in her chest, and she's tempted to text back.

She turns off her phone and tries not to think of him, but it's useless.

His scent lingers on her body, and it's all she can do to not get under the covers and touch herself until she screams his name.

She's losing her mind.

She walks in the rain, shivering until she reaches her car. Stepping inside, she tries to turn it on, praying that it'll work.

But it doesn't.

She screams, pounding her hands on the steering wheel until they ache.

GERARD PICKS HER UP MONDAY.

He's not pleased, to say the least.

"What's your problem?" she finally snaps at him as they reach the parking lot. "Tired from not doing your job?"

It was the wrong thing to say. His hand reaches out, lightning fast, and connects with her face. Her cheek slams into the passenger window, momentarily stunning her.

"You stupid *cunt*," he snarls, as she scrambles out of the passenger door, almost falling on her face.

"What is *wrong* with you?" she shrieks, covering her cheek with her hand, her face burning. "Don't you ever touch me!"

"You almost made me lose my job! You ratted on me, you bitch!"

He takes a step closer, and she takes one back, her feet sliding on the icy concrete.

"Ratted on you?!" she repeats. "What are you talking about?"

"Fifty thousand isn't worth shit! You told Porter I was harassing you?"

None of his words make sense, and she takes another step back. "Fifty thousand? *What*?"

"Aw, fuck it!" He shouts, and she's never been so confused in her life. "Just don't fucking tell him, okay?"

The man is losing it in front of her, and it takes a moment to understand what he's referring to.

"Fifty thousand...dollars? He paid you?"

She's going to throw up.

Horror creeps up her spine.

He paid off Gerard to get close to you.

"Look, look," and suddenly he's panicked, his face pale. "I'm sorry. I shouldn't have hit you. Please don't tell him. God, I fucked up!" His face is red from screaming and his eyes are wild with fear.

"Erik paid you?" she asks, her voice barely above a whisper.

He shakes his head. "No. No. I'm done."

Her head spins, her cheek burns, and nothing makes sense.

She runs into the building, unsure of what to do.

But she knows she needs to speak with Erik immediately.

CHAPTER 23

ERIK

HE SEES EVERYTHING.

He's in the security room tampering with footage when he glances at the camera feed in the parking lot.

He watches Gerard hit her.

The chair crashes into the wall, and his fist connects with a monitor.

CHAPTER 24

ELLIE

"Miss Winters! What happened to your face? Are you alright?" The horror on Doctor Porter's face matches how she feels, but she flashes him a polite smile.

"I slipped on ice," she says quickly, as Gerard follows in, his chest heaving. "Nothing major."

"Nonsense. Gerard, please find Miss Winters an ice pack."

The guard is all too happy to leave, hurrying through the set of double doors.

"Are you ready to meet the other inmate? We'll be assessing him together. Then we can discuss Erik."

His name sends a shiver down her spine, but she agrees, following the doctor down to the Beta ward.

She rattles off her list of questions, documenting her notes, but she's not truly present in her assessment. By the time the session is over, her mind replays every conversation she's had with Erik.

You should know by now I can do anything.

If he has enough money to buy off Gerard, who else could he bribe? Doctor Porter? Another guard?

"Are you alright?" Doctor Porter asks for a second time. "You seem a little...distracted."

She shakes her head. "Fine, really. Just a little dizzy from the fall."

He frowns, but doesn't press the issue. There's a knock on the office door, and Gerard pokes his head in.

"Erik says he doesn't feel well," he informs the doctor. "Says he wants to cancel the session with the Ome—Miss Winters."

Alarm bells ring in her head.

She knows, she just *knows* Erik saw what happened with Gerard.

"That's fine," she says quickly. "I have to work on reports, anyway."

But when Doctor Porter isn't looking, she sends off a quick text message.

Did you pay him off?

She doesn't expect him to answer her.

But by the end of the day, her phone buzzes with a simple reply.

I do what I have to do, baby.
Always.

CHAPTER 25

ERIK

Jealousy is a powerful emotion.

And when someone touches what's his, that jealousy turns into a putrid rage.

He refuses to see her, as painful as it is, because he doesn't have time to explain to her why he did what he did.

There's still too much left to do.

Doctor Porter's office is put to good use as he prints out what he needs, placing it all into a manilla envelope.

He hopes that she'll understand.

And if she doesn't...

She'll just have to accept it.

The spare cord he swiped from the desk sits under his pillow, waiting for the right time to strike.

But he has to bide his time and make sure everything is in place.

He refuses to see her for three days.

For three *fucking days*.

It's torture, and his cock is rock hard, desperate to be inside her.

He sends the text to Gerard in the evening, long after Ellie and Doctor Porter have left. Her scent still lingers, and he inhales it greedily.

Let's talk. Another fifty thousand.

The guard is in his room in less than a minute, shutting the cell door behind him.

"Fifty thousand," Erik insists, towering over him.

"What do you need?" Gerard does his best to not sound intimidated, but he can practically smell the Beta's fear.

"I want you to tell me something."

The other man's mouth drops open in surprise. "Tell you what?"

"Why you hit her."

Gerard pales as he stutters out an explanation.

"I—it was an accident. I—"

"Bullshit," the Alpha hisses. "You touched what's *mine*. You *hurt* her."

"No, I didn't—"

"You never protected her from me!" Erik snarls, his hand slamming into the side of the wall. "You threw her to the wolves because she was an *Omega*. Because you thought she was less than you."

Rage bubbles in him the longer Gerard sputters and makes excuses. "No, I swear—"

But the Beta reaches for his weapon, and Erik wraps the cord around his neck, pulling tightly.

There's hardly a struggle. Gerard's hands fly to his neck, pulling desperately, but Erik watches as his face turns purple with satisfaction.

"This is what you deserve," he murmurs with one last pull, "for hurting what's mine."

Gerard dies unceremoniously, spittle pooling out of his mouth as he hits the cell floor with a *thud*.

The first part of the plan is done.
The second part will be trickier.
And the final part...
That will be quite a spectacle.

CHAPTER 26

ELLIE

SOMETHING'S WRONG.

She can feel it in her bones as she readies in the morning, covering up the mark on her cheek with concealer. Doctor Porter has been driving her every day, and the car rides have been pleasant. She kept the incident with Gerard from him, in case the truth comes out about what she's been doing with Erik.

But today feels...off.

The sky rages, the gray clouds a thick blanket over the earth. The wind howls louder than usual, and the air is thick and gloomy.

She can't ignore the feeling of dread in her chest.

And she hasn't seen Erik in *days*.

He doesn't send any texts. He doesn't call.

And that should be a good thing, but it's not.

She's in the eye of the storm, waiting for whatever awful consequences Erik will give.

To Gerard. To her.

She doesn't know.

And to make it worse, her cramps are back with a vengeance, slick staining every liner she brought. She struggles through each painful blow, doing her best not to focus on the desperate longing in her soul.

Alpha Alpha Alpha

The frantic knocking at her door startles her. It's the normal time Doctor Porter picks her up, but his panicked pounding is *not.*

She opens the door to see his face, pale and stressed.

"What's wrong?" she asks, fear pulling at her chest.

"Gerard's dead."

She freezes.

Oh no.

"What?" It's barely a whisper, but the doctor hears her.

"He hung himself. I found him this morning," he says, his expression pained.

Her mouth opens and closes, unable to process what she's heard. "He *killed* himself?"

"Yes, in the security room. With a power cord."

"Oh, my God."

"We haven't told the inmates yet. I was wondering if you'd like to come with me. I'm sure they heard the sirens, but I haven't broken the news to them yet."

"I...yes, we should go," she stammers.

She doesn't want to go. She wants to run away screaming from Green Woods forever.

But Doctor Porter has been nothing but kind to her, and she won't leave him to bear this alone.

Please, please don't let Erik be behind this.

In the brief car ride, she prays to every deity and God she knows, begging for him to not be involved.

"I'll talk to Erik myself," she says, walking towards the double doors. A police car is still in the parking lot, and Doctor Porter nods as he looks towards the officers.

"Wait inside. I'll be in shortly, Ellie."

A cramp hits her, but she breathes through it, walking as quickly as she can through the double doors.

His scent surrounds her, calling to her, but rage overpowers her need.

She doesn't wait for Doctor Porter.

Instead, she rushes down the hallway, down the stairs, and to his cell, breathing heavily.

She doesn't have a key, so she just stands outside the door, tears blurring her vision.

But to her surprise, the door unlocks from the *inside*. It swings open, and he smiles at her with a crooked grin. Her pussy clenches, but she forces herself to remain focused.

"Gerard's dead," she spits. "But you knew that already."

He raises an eyebrow and opens the door wider. "I missed you too, baby," he purrs. "Come on in. Make yourself at home."

"Did you—" But as she glances around, she freezes. His bed is nothing but a musty cot, with a ratted blanket on top. Books pile on the floor near the door, and a black cell phone sits perched on top of one of them.

There's not even a toilet.

"You've been living like this for three years?" she whispers, turning around slowly.

He only smiles wider, showing off slightly crooked white teeth. "Don't worry, baby. They're kind enough to give me a shower and bathroom break every day." He reaches out a hand and gently touches her cheek. He moves it away when she winces. "Fuck. I was hoping he didn't hit you that badly."

She takes a step back, putting herself in the open doorway. "You knew what he did."

"Of course," he replies. "He touched what's *mine*."

She backs out of the doorway, and he follows her steps. "He killed himself." The statement comes out more like a question, and he smirks.

125

"With a power cord, too. Interesting."

"Oh, God," she whispers. "No. No, you didn't, *please.*" She's frozen as he reaches out to cradle her face.

"Baby, you don't need to be scared. I took care of him for you." His lips are dangerously close to hers, his minty breath washing over her. "I'll always take care of you, sweetheart."

His lips touch hers, briefly, and she drowns in the sensation. He kisses her fiercely, his tongue invading her mouth, and she moans into the kiss.

She could do this forever.

Alpha cares for us. Alpha protects us.

He's the one to break the kiss, his mouth finding her neck. She puts her hands in his hair as he kisses down her throat, nuzzling at her gland. "I'm leaving tonight," she says, shakily. "I quit, today."

That stops him, and she can feel his lips curl into a smile. "With what car?" He murmurs into her neck as goosebumps appear on her flesh. "I made sure it wouldn't power on."

She shoves him away, rage replacing her arousal. "*What?*"

He shrugs. "Your model of car has always been the easiest to de-program. Lucky for me."

The room spins. She's going to pass out.

"You didn't," she whispers. "Please. Please tell me you didn't."

"I did what I had to do, baby."

She closes her eyes, unable to look at his face as she stammers out her next words. "And the fifty thousand?"

"It was actually a hundred thousand altogether. Had to get that extra set of keys."

Too many emotions flood through her at once, and she lets out a choked sob. "You're *insane,*" she says through the tears. "I can't be a part of this anymore. This is done. All of it."

But as she looks at him, he just stares back, amused.

"Sorry, sweetheart. This is a two-person decision now. And I vote no."

He takes a step closer, arms outstretched, and she shoves at his chest with all her strength. He barely stumbles, but she staggers back at the force of her movement.

"I'm *done*. You're fucking *crazy*," she snarls. "This was a mistake. Stay away from me."

Footsteps come near, and she turns and runs down the hallway toward the sound, almost crashing directly into Doctor Porter.

"Miss Winters?" He asks, confused. "What are you doing down here?"

"I have to leave Green Woods. I'm so sorry." She takes off running, ignoring the doctor calling after her.

She has to get out of this town, consequences be damned.

LITA DOESN'T ANSWER HER PHONE.

She's losing signal as she stands awkwardly in one corner of the cabin, desperate for help.

She contemplates calling the police, but she knows they wouldn't give her a ride back to Los Angeles.

And the cramps are unbearable.

She ends up spending the day soaking in the bath, ignoring the calls from Doctor Porter.

By evening, her head is so foggy she's barely able to answer the phone. She only wants to crawl into bed, bury herself under the covers, and sleep away the pain.

But before she can do that, Lita calls her, and she answers almost immediately.

"Can you come get me?" she croaks, her fevered mind panicking. "Please."

"Oh shit, Ellie. What happened?"

"I can't...I need to leave," she whispers. "Please. Please help me, Lita."

"Are you safe?! Do I need to call the police?"

"No police," Ellie chokes out. "No. Just you, please. My car broke down."

"Absolutely," she says. "I'll leave in an hour. Stay safe for me, okay? Promise me."

She could cry with relief, knowing she'll be away from this monstrous place in a few hours. "Yes. I'll be safe. I promise."

She packs her bags and waits in bed for Lita, eventually drifting off into a fitful sleep.

CHAPTER 27

ERIK

HE *REALLY* DIDN'T WANT TO TRACK HER PHONE.

He had paired his app with hers while she slept that night in the hospital, and he vowed to never use it unless he absolutely had to.

Like right now.

Clever girl, getting a ride from her boss.

But it only takes a few phone calls to cancel the trip.

He sees the incoming text from Lita as it appears on Ellie's screen:

I'm so sorry, my brother's been in a car crash. Can't come tonight.

Of course, once Lita gets to the hospital, she'll realize it was a hoax.

But it buys him just enough time.

He knew Ellie would come to accuse him and try to end what they have.

But they're more alike than she realizes, and he plans on showing her exactly how.

There's a more pressing issue, though.

He could smell the start of her Heat as she stood in his cell. Her skin was clammy against his lips, her skin flushed as he touched her.

She even tasted different. She was sweeter, somehow.

He's grateful for the suppressants they inject inside him, as he'll still be lucid when he takes her.

His Rut is inevitable, his skin clammy and hot as well, but he's able to think clearly.

And when Doctor Porter leads him into his office to deliver the bad news, he's able to stay as calm as possible.

"Sorry I haven't been here all day," he apologizes, genuinely concerned. "Unfortunately, we lost Gerard. I can't go into specifics, but he won't be working here anymore."

He nods, and the doctor continues.

"Ellie Winters will also not be with us anymore," he sighs. "She quit this morning, likely due to the stress of what happened with Gerard."

He internally scoffs.

That's not why.

"That's unfortunate," he says evenly. "She was good at her job."

Doctor Porter gives him a pointed look. "She was good for you as well. You've done phenomenal work with me since she came here. You've opened up and been more comfortable talking about who you are."

He shrugs, but he knows it's true.

She's the first person who made him want to *exist* again.

He knew the consequences of avenging Cassandra's death, and he had accepted them, even before he killed the three Alphas.

Something so evil could only be repaid with a heinous act, and he fully expected to be put to death himself. When he turned himself in to save the innocent Beta suspect, he accepted that he would have only a few years left to live.

But money had its way of talking, and he negotiated for a lifelong sentence, instead.

And he had never, ever expected to find a mate.

But then she had walked in, stubborn, beautiful, and determined to do good.

And the more he found out about her, the more he realized they were meant to be.

Soulmates.

"I am more comfortable, because of her," he admits. "She makes me want to do things better. To be better."

The admission stuns both of them, and the doctor smiles. "I loved having her here."

"Me too."

I loved having her here. I loved her.

I love her.

As a monster, love shouldn't be in his vocabulary.

But with Ellie...

He wants to give her whatever shredded part of his soul he has left.

He wants to love her until she can't see straight, and she realizes how perfect she is.

He wants her to realize that even with her trauma and pain, she's still worthy of having someone care for her.

Whatever is left of his heart belongs to her.

His Alpha roars in approval.

HE DOESN'T WANT TO HURT ANYONE ELSE UNLESS HE absolutely has to. And even then, it would only be to subdue them, not cause permanent damage.

But things are messier than they need to be.

There's an officer posted outside his cell, one much more competent than Gerard. One who happens to be an Alpha.

A possessive growl rises in his chest as he smells the Alpha's putrid essence, and all he can think about is Ellie.

He needs to claim her before anyone else can.

Checking his phone, he's able to see any outgoing calls or text messages she's made.

There's one to Doctor Porter, sent only seconds ago, which gives him pause.

I need your help. Please.

No, that simply won't do.

He disables her phone, blocking out her signal entirely.

He waits for the Alpha guard to make his rounds, listening for his footsteps to fade as he heads towards the Beta ward.

Then he makes his escape, heading back towards the security room and to the circuit breakers.

CHAPTER 28

ELLIE

<small>HER HOPE DIES AS SOON AS HER PHONE STOPS WORKING.</small>

It's completely disabled, only seconds after she sends the text to Doctor Porter.

She knows Erik's behind it. He has to be.

And he might even be behind the reason Lita wasn't able to come.

Did he hurt someone else?

She doubles over in the bed, clutching her stomach, breathing through the painful cramps.

She's a mess. Slick drips down her, sticky and wet. Her body is so flushed that her hair sticks to her forehead.

And she's aroused.

So. Fucking. Aroused.

Her clit throbs painfully, begging to be touched. Her nipples are hard as diamonds, and entirely too painful as they rub against the rough fabric of her shirt.

She has only one chance left.

And she hopes beyond hope that Doctor Porter is still in the building and can give her a ride out of this hellhole.

And maybe it's her fever, or her delirium that has her walking an hour later towards the facility, in a trance-like state. Maybe it's the Heat she's put off for so long that carries her legs easily, the cold air not affecting her.

Or maybe it's something deeper.

But by the time she's past the trees and near the parking lot, she realizes something is wrong.

The power's blown out there, again.

But sirens fill the air, and the blades of a helicopter overhead snap her back to reality.

And she can smell him, suddenly, his scent entirely too strong for this far outside the building.

He's escaped.

She turns around, the spell broken, and *runs*.

PRESENT DAY

HER HEAD THROBS. IT'S BEYOND PAIN; IT'S A BLADE OF FIRE, and even in the darkness of the dusty basement it's still too bright.

She's soaked herself through, her pants a sopping mess, slick everywhere.

She sets the knife down next to her as quietly as she can.

Would she even use it on him? Could she?

Don't hurt Alpha!

But she doesn't have a lot of options as the wind howls and his scent grows stronger.

She either overpowers him or he takes her.

It's as simple as that.

But that decision may have already been made for her,

134

because she falls to her side, clutching her stomach, willing herself to breathe as quietly as possible.

She spent her last Heat in isolation, away from any Alphas.

But now her body screams for him, her heart aches for him...

But her mind says no.

She can't. They can't.

There's a *thud* as objects slam against the wall upstairs. Eyes closed, she prays it's not the table and chairs she used as barricades.

Please, she thinks. *Please go away.*

Heavy footsteps walk overhead, and she crawls into the furthest corner of the basement, away from the door.

"Sweetheart." His voice is low and silky behind the wall. "Are you in here?"

Alpha!

Help me Alpha!

But she bites her tongue, willing herself to stay quiet.

The pain is excruciating, and she huddles into a ball, willing this night to be over.

"Baby. Do I really have to break this door down?"

He's so calm, his voice so gentle, that she almost gives herself away.

Alpha would make it better.

Alpha could help me.

She screams into the crook of her elbow, desperation and need slicing through her body, her cunt spasming.

Her head pounds in time with her rapidly beating heart.

She barely registers the kicks at the door, instead staring straight ahead into the darkness, his delicious scent growing closer.

She hears him curse, then his powerful arms are around her, hoisting her up. "Sweetheart," he whispers. "I'm here. You don't need to be scared anymore."

"Hurts," she whimpers, angry at herself for being so weak.

"I know, baby. But I'm going to make it better, okay?"

She loses her balance, falling face first into his chest, but his massive hands reach out, holding her in place. He's no longer in his prison scrubs. Instead, he's wearing a dark sweater and denim jeans.

She drifts in and out of awareness as he leads her back toward the stairs, but he stops to pick something up. "Really? A knife, Ellie?" he chides her. "You should know that wouldn't be enough to stop me."

She groans, desperate to stay lucid. "Did you hurt Doctor Porter?"

"Absolutely not," he says, scooping her into his arms. Her limbs are made of lead, and she has no strength to fight him anymore. "He's a good man. I promise you, he's unharmed."

"But what about Lita..."

"A few phone calls. No one is hurt," he assures her. "You also already told her not to bother and you're coming back at the end of the week. Honestly, you act like I'm a murderer."

He chuckles at his joke as he carries her back up the stairs and into the front room. "I can't ever forgive you for this," she murmurs

Laying her gently on the worn couch, he places his lips to her forehead. "You're burning up. It's not safe for you to go through your Heat by yourself. Any Alpha could take advantage of you. I'm protecting you, sweetheart."

She could kill him at that moment.

The *audacity*.

"They're going to come for you," she tries again, and she hears him scoff in the darkness.

"Actually, they all think I'm an hour away by now," he calls, rummaging through the bedroom. "Which gives me ample time to prepare."

The power switches back on, and the tiny overhead light

shines down on her. She tries to move, but her limbs don't cooperate.

"Time to prepare for what?" she croaks out.

"Your Heat, sweetheart. Are these all the blankets you have?" He walks back into her view and her heart stutters.

He's disturbingly handsome in the black v-neck sweater that shows off the definition of his muscles. The dark blue denim of his pants is perfectly tailored to his hips and thighs, giving him a polished look. With his dark hair styled, he looks like a model.

It's not fair.

He repeats his question, but she closes her eyes, refusing to face reality anymore. He takes her hand, his palm engulfing hers, and she sighs against his touch.

No matter how much she hates it, her body calls to him.

She *needs* him.

Their fingers intertwine, and she hears a soft rumbling sound.

He's purring for her.

"I'm going to make it better," he vows, smoothing his hand over her clammy forehead. "I promise."

"The only thing that would make this better is your disappearing from my life," she grits out, even as she grips his hand tighter.

He leans over her, his purr growing louder, and scoops her into his arms. "Too late for that," he sighs. "I'm all in now. I don't break out of prison for just anyone."

"Oh, God," she groans, as he carries her, along with the blankets, back to the bedroom. "How can you make jokes at a time like this?"

His grip on her hardens, his fingers holding on deep enough to bruise. "It's either that, or I lose control and fuck you senseless. You tell me which way we're doing this, baby."

She can't stop the moan that escapes her, because she wants him. She wants him inside her so badly she might die.

It's his cock or perishing in anguish from need.

"After this," she croaks out, grabbing at his sweater and pulling him down. "We're done."

He growls, pressing her deeper against the mattress. "We'll see, baby."

CHAPTER 29

ERIK

HE LOVES HER.

And whether or not she's ready to admit it, she needs him.

Her scent changed the moment he entered the basement. The sourness of her fear evaporated into sweet joy.

It was lust mixed with care, tenderness blended with need.

He knows she holds resentment, and he doesn't blame her.

After all, they met under "questionable" circumstances.

But the suppressants that pump through his veins are strong enough to keep himself under control as she desperately latches to him, pulling him on top of her in the bed.

He keeps his inner Alpha under control, careful to stay in tune with what she needs. And right now, she needs him to touch her.

He'll never tire of kissing her. It's the most natural thing in the world. His lips meld with hers, and she sighs against his mouth.

"Omega," he murmurs, between kisses.

"Please," she begs. "Make it stop hurting, Erik."

He doesn't need to be told twice. He yanks down her sweats, exposing her overheated body to the cool air. He reaches a hand between her legs and wraps the other one around her throat as he plays with her.

She arches into his touch and he squeezes tighter, just to remind her who she belongs to.

As he suspected, she loves it. She soaks his fingers within seconds, and he works her to orgasm shortly after. She comes quietly, his hand still wrapped around her throat, her voice escaping in choked gasps as she rides his hand.

When he finally lets her go, she gasps for air, but a wicked grin spreads across her face.

That's my girl.

"More," she demands, spreading her legs obscenely wide, exposing herself to him. "Inside me. *Please.*"

As her Heat begins, her scent changes. It's fucking irresistible, and he's shucking off his clothes before he can think. His cock finds the entrance to her cunt, and he pushes in, unable to hold back anymore. They both groan in unison as he buries himself in her as deeply as he can, desperate to feel as close to her as possible.

He doesn't hold back. He thrusts into her, fucking her ruthlessly on the bed, claiming her cunt over and over.

"You. Are. *Mine,*" he snarls with every slam of his hips, and she can only nod her head in agreement.

"Yours," she whispers, wrapping her legs around his ass and taking him deeper.

His hand reaches back to her throat, and she gushes her slick down his cock. "You ever try to leave me," he hisses. "I'll hunt you down. You'll never run from me again. Do you understand me, Omega?"

He squeezes too tight until her beautiful face turns pink, but she agrees. His mouth places punishing kisses on her throat, sucking bruises into every inch of her delicate skin.

Bite her, his Alpha snarls. *Take her.*

And it's so, so tempting to do it. He wants to sink his teeth into her like a fucking animal and break the delicate skin of her gland, tying her soul to his forever.

One snap of his jaw and he could force every inch of her heart and mind to meld with his.

But whatever part of his heart is left knows that it's inherently *wrong.*

He needs her permission, and that will make it even more delicious when she finally realizes what he's known since the first day he met her.

They're soulmates.

He's sure to leave bruises with how tight he's choking her, but she begins to spasm on his cock, milking him, and he comes with a roar. She follows suit, her eyes rolling into the back of her head as she falls over the edge, her body vibrating from the intensity of her release.

It's fucking heaven.

His balls tighten as his cock swells, and this time, it's different.

He's locked inside her so deeply, he's not sure they'll ever separate.

They pass out together, spooning just like the night in the hospital bed.

His Omega is freezing.

He's slipped out of her sometime in the night, and he can *hear* her teeth chattering as he wraps her in more blankets. His own body is burning up, the symptom of a violent Rut, and he slips out of bed to prepare what she needs before they both lose control again.

She's delirious when he comes back, her eyes glazed over as she regards him with confusion.

"Alpha?" she asks quietly, her voice soft and sweet.

And he wishes, more than anything, that she would share that same tenderness with him once she returns to her senses.

It most likely won't be for a while, if ever, after what he's done.

"Drink," he says, holding a water bottle to her lips. She obeys without complaint, downing half the container at once.

"Thank you, Alpha," she whispers. Her eyes are tender and full of longing, emotion shining through. "I need you, Erik. Touch me."

He cups her face in his hands and kisses her deeply.

"There's nothing I want to do more. You understand I'll always take care of you, baby?" He whispers against her lips. "Always."

Her fingers run through his hair, tugging at the scalp, and he groans.

"Love me, Alpha," she murmurs.

"Always," he growls. "I'll never stop."

She won't remember his confession afterward, but for now, her pupils widen, and she gazes at him with wonder.

He expected the second round to be rough, but he's gentle with her, pushing her back down so they're on their sides. His cock barely fits inside her, but the residual slick and cum lubricates him perfectly.

He thrusts once, then twice, into her as she gasps, backing her ass up against him.

"You're so tight like this," he whispers in her ear. "So fucking *small*. You're such a good girl, taking it."

His hands find her nipples and gently tug, and she falls over the edge, slick staining the bed. She grips his cock, rocking back and forth on his knot, gasping his name. He continues his assault, finding her clit and rubbing in slow circles as she spasms on his knot.

He pumps her full of cum until she stops moving, her body giving out.

She falls asleep before he does, and he whispers promises into her ear. He tells her secrets he knows she won't remember.

He loves her.

He's sorry it had to be like this.

He wants to be better for her.

She's everything he wishes he could be.

And as he drifts asleep, he notices her scent changing back to its normal sweetness.

Her Heat is ending almost as soon as it began.

CHAPTER 30

ELLIE

ERIK *SNORES.*

In any other circumstance it would be hilarious, but in this one, not so much.

His arm is slung around her lazily, holding her close in an iron grip. The sheets are ruined, stained with slick and cum, and she shifts uncomfortably in the mess.

She needs a shower, then she can figure out what her next steps are.

And why the hell aren't the police banging down the front door?

She tiptoes down the hall and peeks at the front door, which he barricaded again with the same furniture. The door sits in the frame at an awkward angle, warped from his ministrations the other night. Sunlight shines in through the small windows, the sky beautiful and blue.

The storm is over, and now she can finally plan her escape.

Much to her dismay, he locked the basement door, which likely holds her phone.

Don't panic. You'll figure this out.

She quickly washes up in the bathroom, rinsing away the scent and evidence of their lust.

When she turns the tap off, she exhales in relief as his subtle snoring continues.

It's time to leave.

But as she throws on her clothes as quietly as possible, anxiety grows in her stomach. Lying on the bed with his eyes closed and lips slightly parted, he's disturbingly handsome. The lines in his troubled face are smoothed, and he looks at peace.

He looks...happy.

She chews her lip and stares at him, watching his chest rise and fall as he sleeps deeply.

Her heart breaks as she faces the truth.

He's a fugitive.

And if she stays any longer, she's an accomplice.

She won't tell anyone where he is. It will give him a head start, and he will go wherever he needs to go.

He belongs in prison, but she doesn't want to see him behind bars again.

"Damn it," she whispers under her breath, fighting the emotions that bubble to the surface.

We can't leave Alpha!

The longer she watches him sleep, the more her resolve fades.

But she *has* to leave him, regardless of what her inner Omega screams at her.

He discarded his clothes on the floor, his dark jeans strewn haphazardly next to a blanket.

She freezes when she sees the small electronic device hanging halfway out of the pocket.

His cellphone sits within reach.

With shaky fingers, she moves as quietly as she can until the phone is in her hand.

The snores continue.

Gripping it like a lifeline, she backs out of the room and runs to the front room, cupping the phone tightly to her chest.

She holds her breath as she touches the screen.

Nothing.

Please don't be dead, she thinks as the pushes she power button. The screen finally comes to life, and she attempts to unlock it.

Nothing.

"Please, please," she whispers, finally tapping *Emergency Call.* She can think of something to say. She doesn't have to mention Erik. She can just...

"Baby."

She shrieks and drops the phone as she turns around to see him only inches from her, fully dressed. He looks at the phone, now feet away on the wood floor, then back at her with a raised eyebrow.

"I thought we were past this part, baby." He takes another step closer, and she instinctively moves back.

He's as striking as ever, with day-old stubble growing on his pale skin. His dark hair is mussed yet still stylish, layers falling into his dark eyes.

His scent calls to her, subtle and dark, and she fights the urge to throw herself into his arms.

"I have to leave, Erik," she whispers. "I have to go back home."

His expression doesn't change. "I'm your home now."

"No," she says louder, her fists clenching. "I have a job. A life."

"You can have a job all you want, baby. You can have as many as you fucking well please, but it will not be in Los Angeles."

"You're out of your *mind*," she growls.

"You'll finally have a family. We'll make one, together."

He says it calmly, like it's a simple plan they've already decided on. But it's a punch to her gut, and she gasps, tears filling her eyes.

She hasn't had a family since she was seventeen. And above all, it's what she wants.

A place to belong.

"Fuck *you*," she hisses instead, blinking back tears. "You can't do this to me."

A step closer. "It's already been done," he whispers, his fingers caressing her cheek. "You know what this is. You've felt it since we first met."

Soulmates.

She knows he's right, that beyond the attraction is something that she can't explain through biology.

Deep in her heart, she knows he's her mate.

"I refuse it," she whispers painfully, refusing to meet his eyes.

Her conscience won't let her.

But he's still as calm as before, even with her resistance. "I had a feeling you'd say that," he sighs. His fingers lightly tilt her chin up to look at him. "You're going to have to forgive me for this last part, my love."

Before she can marvel at the term of endearment, his other hand shoots up and touches her neck with a sharp sting. With wide eyes, she watches as he removes the syringe, her mind sluggish as she struggles to remain standing.

"It was the only way to do this," he whispers in her ear as she loses her balance. He keeps her upright until he moves her towards the couch, laying her gently on the pillows.

"You..." she slurs. "What..."

The overhead light spins in circles around her. She keeps her gaze fixed on the ceiling as he speaks.

"They use it on us when we act up," he says casually. "I

147

made sure you only got half, baby. Just relax. You need to give me time to pack our things, okay? Then I've got to start the car."

It doesn't work, she thinks wildly. *You ruined the battery.*

But no words come out, and she eventually drifts into a drug-induced slumber.

CHAPTER 31

ERIK

His list of reasons to apologize keeps growing.

But hopefully, what he plans to give her will be enough to warrant just an ounce of her forgiveness.

She sleeps quietly as he packs their belongings in her duffel bags. He grabs whatever water and non-perishable food he finds in the kitchen.

Just like a vacation, he thinks wildly to himself. *That's where we're going. A family vacation.*

He wasn't lying when he offered her a family. His only family was Cassandra after they lost their parents, and when she was ripped away, it blew a hole in his heart.

Ellie knows the same pain. She knows what it's like to blame yourself and to crave a sense of belonging that never comes.

He'll give it to her. He'll fill her with as many babies as she fucking wants.

Or, if she wants it to just be the two of them, that's fine as well.

That conversation is a long way ahead, though.

———

The car is easy enough to reprogram, and it purrs to life the minute he pushes the power button. He tucked Ellie neatly in the passenger seat, and she sleeps deeply as they say goodbye to Green Woods forever.

Their trip takes them a few hours north, which is perfect timing. He placed the manilla folder in Ellie's lap and he waits anxiously for her to wake up.

He missed driving. He forgot what a change of scenery looks like, and he takes in the mountains, trees, and bodies of water as they travel.

Finally, she stirs. She sits upright in her seat, her mouth hanging open in shock.

"Ellie," he says, as she fumbles with her seat belt. They're on the freeway, and she sure as shit better not unbuckle herself and try to open the door. "*Omega.* Calm down."

But she does the exact opposite. "Are you adding kidnapping to your list of charges now?" She spits. She glances at a freeway sign and frowns. "*Where* are we going?"

"Look in the envelope," he replies, keeping his eyes on the road. "Look in the envelope, and it will explain everything."

"There's nothing to explain," she insists. "Let me out. Or I'll start screaming."

He rolls his eyes. "Just open the damn envelope, Ellie."

She bites her lip, her anger deepening her scent. Her hand dances over the envelope, her finger stopping at the top.

"Just trust me," he murmurs, glancing at her. "Please."

She must see something in his eyes or feel his sincerity, because she slowly opens it, allowing the papers to fall into her lap. There are minutes of silence as she reads through each one.

He carefully compiled each paper and spent his nights in Doctor Porter's office, researching and pulling up records.

And, of course, he hacked into databases when necessary.

He only hopes it will be enough. He can't change her past, but he can give her something she's wanted.

He can give her answers.

They're on another freeway by the time she speaks. "You found him?" Her voice is broken, barely above a whisper.

"Ronald Dennis. Yes."

"He..." she turns the papers over again, scanning. "He went to a hospital the night of the accident."

"He had injuries similar to that of a car accident. Two weeks later, his truck was in a body shop for damage consistent with a head-on collision."

She's silent until he hears her tears hitting the papers. "This is him," she chokes out. "You found him."

"I finally used my powers for good," he murmurs.

"I can't believe you did this," she says.

"Life doesn't give us a lot of answers," he murmurs. "I was glad I could give you at least one."

To his surprise, she takes the hand he rests on his thigh, intertwining their fingers. He keeps one hand on the steering wheel as he squeezes her hand.

"Where are we going?" She asks again.

"We're going to pay him a visit," he says. "And whatever happens after that is up to you."

CHAPTER 32

ELLIE

SHE'S SO DUMBFOUNDED BY WHAT HE'S DONE THAT SHE can't even thank him.

She just continues to stare at the papers in disbelief, double-checking to make sure it truly is him.

The picture on his license is eerily similar to the brief glance she had of him the day of the accident.

But she needs to be sure.

Erik accessed every stop light camera between the roads, finding the license plates and tracking each one. He located the vehicle owners, researched hospital records, and did much more than the police bothered to do. Based on the skid marks, the driver was most likely drunk.

"How long did this take you?" she asks finally, absorbing every detail. "Even the police didn't do this much work."

Erik did all of this in a week while incarcerated.

"It took too long," he says. "I wanted to get you the information as soon as possible. Even if..."

She repeats his words, and he clears his throat.

"Even if you didn't want me."

She almost scoffs at the absurdity of his statement.

Of course she wants him. Her body calls to him.

Her inner Omega screams for him.

Her heart longs for him.

The only part that's hesitant is her mind. Her rationale, and everything that allows her to stay in control, is threatened by being near him.

Her shoulder throbs, her gland delicate after the abuse from his mouth.

He could have claimed her there, in the isolated cabin, but he chose not to.

It would have been easier for her if he did. Then she would have no reason to leave his side.

She wonders if, in his own way, he's offering her a choice.

She squeezes his hand tighter.

Ronald's home is unkempt, to say the least.

Hidden down a winding road overgrown with weeds, the small trailer has paint chipping on the outside, along with a front lawn with grass as tall as Ellie.

They're in the middle of nowhere in a town not much larger than Green Woods.

There's a vehicle parked to the side, and she freezes when she sees a dusty red truck.

"That's his truck," she whispers as Erik parks the car. "Holy shit, that's the truck that hit is."

He squeezes her hand in reassurance. "So, how do you want to do this, baby?" He flashes her a smirk, his eyes dark and malicious. "You want to do the honors, or me?"

A better person would walk away, she thinks.

A better person could forgive.

But right now, she doesn't want to be the better person.

153

"If anything happens to him," she says slowly. "It's on *my* terms. It's *my* decision."

His smirk turns into a wicked grin, and he growls in approval. "That's my girl. Lead the way, sweetheart."

They walk up the porch, the wooden steps rotting and warping. Her mind is clouded with indecision and anxiety. Erik walks behind her, his scent enveloping her. She can feel the pride radiating off him in waves, and she uses his faith in her as strength.

She stops short of the door, a simple wire screen on a faded frame.

The man who killed her mother and sister is behind that door.

The monster who left them to burn alive, and left Ellie to save herself, is mere feet away from her.

As she knocks on the door, she realizes there are different kinds of monsters.

Erik has a moral compass, however warped it may be.

But Ronald...

He doesn't even have a heart.

"I'm right here," Erik whispers behind her. "And whatever happens, I love you."

His confession stuns her, but she doesn't have time to process his words as the door swings open. A man with bloodshot eyes stares at her as he shakes on wobbly legs, dressed in a stained white shirt and cargo shorts.

And the *stench*. He smells like death, a combination of tobacco and sickly sweet alcohol with a hint of garlicky body order.

He's an Alpha, that much is clear. As he senses her Omega essence, he leans down and breathes his putrid breath at her.

"You the girl?" He slurs, his chapped lips forming into a smile. His teeth are filled with the darkness of chewing tobacco, and everything in her wants to run away.

This is the face of a monster.

But with Erik beside her, she holds on to her courage and speaks. "Are you Ronald?" Her voice is more confident than she feels.

"Yeah. S'me. You're that Omega. Truck girl."

Her head is spinning because she realizes he *recognizes* her.

There's no doubting it now. He was driving the vehicle that hit her family.

"You killed my mother and sister." Her heart pounds wildly in her chest as she faces the man responsible for her nightmares and self-loathing. He leans against the doorway and sneers.

"You made it out, right? I saw you crawlin'. Figured you'd be fine."

The more he speaks, the greater her nausea grows. "You saw me get out of the car?"

Erik growls behind her, and the Alpha flicks his glassy eyes towards him. "Sure did. I had to drive away quickly, though. Was drinking and all that."

She's shaking, but she doesn't know if it's from agony or anger.

"You left three women out there to die. And two did."

Ronald simply shrugs. "Well, no one's going to believe you. Now get the fuck off my porch, bitch. Before I get my shotgun and shoot the both of you."

Erik pushes in front of her and launches himself at Ronald with a roar. The men fall to the cheap floor and she rushes in, yelling. But there's barely a fight, because Erik is on top of him in a second, a pistol in his hands.

"We don't have to—" the other Alpha starts.

"Shut the *fuck* up!" Erik snarls, his pistol pointed at the man's head. "Say one more fucking word and I kill you right here."

She's frozen in shock as she watches Erik take out a zip tie and strap Ronald's wrists together. He hauls him up, then shoves him on a ratty, torn grey couch.

"You okay, baby?" Erik asks her softly, gun still trained on Ronald.

"Yes," she says, walking slowly through the front room. The house stinks of cigarettes and old beer, with butts and cans lining the stained brown carpet. Walls that were once white have years of yellow stains from smoking.

A television with a smashed screen sits in a corner. Microwavable dinners litter the scuffed coffee table.

"You live like this?" she whispers. She looks around a corner to see his shotgun against the back wall.

Erik keeps his gun trained on Ronald, his muscled forearms flexing. "What's it going to be, baby?"

Ronald begins to cry with pathetic whines. His face turns bright red, and he wails like a toddler.

It *infuriates* Ellie.

"Shut up," she hisses, walking until she's only inches from him, but out of Erik's line of fire. "And look at me."

Ugly tears and snot fall down the man's face, but he obeys.

"You killed everyone I held dear. You ruined my *life,*" she snarls. "And you showed no remorse. *Nothing.*"

Erik's scent changes as his pride for her swells. It fuels her to continue.

"Do you know what I do for a living? I try to see the good in the worst types of people—people that some would say are monsters."

Ronald sniffles. "I'm sorry. I truly am."

"What's my name?" she bellows at him. "If you're so sorry, did you bother to even look up the name of your *victims?*" Her screech echoes throughout the house as Ronald sobs.

"I don't—I don't—"

"You have no remorse. There's no saving you. You took two lives, then threw away your own to live like *this.*"

She bites her lip to keep from crying, but her voice chokes up. "No one can help you, Ronald. I hoped I would be able to forgive you when I knew we were coming here. But there's not enough forgiveness in the world to save you."

She takes a step back and looks at Erik, motioning toward his gun. "Give it to me."

Ronald yells, squirming on the couch and attempting to slide off it.

"I said don't *fucking move!*" Erik roars, and the older man freezes.

Ellie walks up to Erik, brushing her hand up to his shoulder. "Give it to me, Erik."

For the first time, he seems uneasy. "You sure, baby? There's no going back from this. Ever."

Ronald's cries become background noise to her as she relives the day of the accident.

The glass cutting into her palms.

Her mom's screams, turning into a warped groan as the flames consume her.

Juliet's skin melting to the leather of the passenger seat...

"I'm sure."

Erik cocks the gun and carefully hands it to her. He wraps his hands around hers and maneuvers the pistol slightly until it's facing perfectly at Ronald's head.

"You just need to pull the trigger, sweetheart."

Her hands shake, and Erik holds her steady. "Will you do it with me?" she whispers, and his hands squeeze tighter.

"Of course." Her finger goes to the trigger and his finger follows. As both their fingers touch the trigger, Erik brings his lips to her ear.

"I'm so proud of you, baby."

Together, they fire.

CHAPTER 33

ERIK

RONALD DIES UNCEREMONIOUSLY, JUST LIKE GERARD. HE slumps over on the couch, a puddle of dark red dripping down his forehead.

He feels no remorse. He deserves none.

But he senses Ellie's shock as she drops the gun, her shirt and hands now stained with blood splatter.

"Erik," she whispers, staring at her hands. "Erik..."

He pulls her into his arms as she shakes. "Don't look at him, baby," he whispers. "It's all done now, okay? You're safe." He presses a kiss on the top of her head. "I promise. I'm here. You're safe, baby, and he'll never hurt you again."

"I killed him," she murmurs into his chest. "I...I could get arrested..."

"No, you won't. I'm going to take care of it all." She lifts her head from his chest, and he wipes the single tear that slides down her cheek. "You're in shock right now. Focus on me, okay? Focus on my scent. I'm with you."

She nods, her eyes glassy. "I killed him."

"You did, sweetheart. And you did the world a fucking favor."

But his girl's not a killer, and he can see the remorse in her eyes, as undeserving as it may be.

He presses his lips to hers, not caring about the blood that stains them both, pushing all of his emotions into her. "I love you," he whispers against her lips. "Can you hold on to that? Until I clean up the mess and get us out of here?"

She won't say it back now, he knows, but she nods anyway. "Yes," she says. "I can hold on to that."

He gives her a smile and kisses her nose. "Get back in the car for me," he says. "Stay there and keep your eyes closed. You don't need to see the rest of this."

Something dark flashes in her eyes as she looks back at the blood on her hands. "Okay. And Erik?" She stops at the doorway, meeting his eyes. "I love you, too. I think I have for a while."

It's the shock, he tells himself. *The adrenaline. She can't know yet.*

But he smiles to himself as he rids the area of any evidence.

———

SHE FELL ASLEEP WHILE SHE WAITED FOR HIM.

Which he's grateful for because he didn't want her to smell or see the smoke of the fire he made.

Burning Ronald and his house down was the best course of action, but he wanted her to stay as far away from it as possible.

He remembers what the fire alarm did to her. He can't imagine how she would react if she witnessed something like this.

Watching her take control of her life was incredible. She

159

commanded the room as she looked the Alpha in the face and told him what he'd done to her.

She was beautiful, bold, and free when he helped her pull the trigger.

And when she confessed her love...

But he refuses to accept she meant it. How could she, after everything?

He's lost in thought as he drives them to their newest destination when she finally wakes up. "Erik?" she asks, dazed.

"Hi, baby," he purrs. "Did you sleep okay?"

She's quiet for a long time. "I slept...peacefully," she finally says. "A deep, dreamless sleep. It's something I haven't had in a very long time."

The corner of his lip quirks up. "I know the feeling," he says. "I've been sleeping that way for the past few nights."

"Lucky you," she quips back.

"Lucky me," he agrees.

They ride in silence for a while, and she watches as the freeway signs appear again. "What's next?" she asks, staring out the window.

"We have reservations for a luxury hotel," he says casually. "Under Mr. And Mrs. Jones."

"We're married now?" she asks incredulously. "Only an hour ago we were accomplices. When did marriage happen?"

He expected her anger, but delights in her humor. "It just makes it easier. We need a place to wash up and rest."

"Hmm. Then what?"

"Then, we talk."

He doesn't mean for it to sound ominous, but he notices her subtle shudder.

CHAPTER 34

ELLIE

SHE'S A MURDERER NOW.

And she harbored a fugitive.

What's next?

We talk.

But what is there to talk about?

She made her choice the minute she pulled the trigger. She altered the course of her future, with him at her side.

Maybe he's changed his mind. Maybe he wants to be on the run by himself.

Or maybe he wants to use her as leverage for the murder in exchange for a lighter sentence if he gets caught.

But she recognizes the signs of shock and tries not to drown in irrational thoughts.

Right now, the only person she trusts is right next to her, driving her electric car through the northwest states.

His scent wraps around her, caressing her with comfort. When he confessed his love, she was sure she heard him wrong, or that he was saying it in the heat of the moment.

But his scent is richer and more potent than it ever was, and she revels in the care.

She loves him too.

He's her family now.

"What are you thinking about?" he asks softly, as they turn off an exit.

"The future," she replies.

She swears she can see the beginning of a smile.

"Me too," he says wistfully.

THE HOT WATER IS HEAVEN ON HER SKIN, BEATING DOWN the last of her nerves and washing away the painful memories of the day.

By the time she emerges from the water, her soul is quieted, her mind calm.

She expected guilt to take over and paralyze her, but instead, a weight is lifted off her shoulders.

Nothing will ever bring her mother and sister back, but she brought a balance to the situation.

She's a vigilante now, just like the Alpha that waits for her in the hotel bedroom.

She steps out in just her towel, and he smiles at her wickedly. Her womb clenches and her nipples harden just from him *looking* at her.

"We're famous, baby," he says, handing her his phone. "They think I abducted you."

Inmate Escaped, Woman Kidnapped, the headline reads. She skims the article and almost laughs at how inaccurate it is.

"They think we're heading to Mexico?" She smiles up at him.

"Well, technically, they think you're in my trunk accompanying me to Mexico."

A week ago, his words would have scared her. But now, a delicious shiver races up her spine.

"Isn't that what you're doing, though? Kidnapping me?"

He takes a step towards her, his dark eyes smoldering. "Is that what you want me to do, Miss Winters? You want the big bad Alpha to take you and steal you away forever?"

She's soaked now, slick dribbling down her thighs. "Ah, I think you do," he purrs. "You can fight me all you want, baby, if that makes you feel better. But I'm not leaving your fucking side."

She looks at the man who liberated her, who did everything he could for her, and smiles.

Then she lets the towel fall.

"Fuck," he hisses, his eyes dropping to her breasts. "You're fucking perfect, Ellie. But if we do this tonight...I won't be able to stop myself."

She hears the unspoken words.

I'll mate you tonight.

"I choose you, Erik," she murmurs. "I want it to be you."

"It'll trigger your Heat, sweetheart. And my Rut." But he's not arguing. Instead, he flashes her a wolfish grin. "You want to fuck this hotel room up? It's going to be violent, baby. I have no more suppressants."

Oh, fuck.

She sinks down to her knees in front of him, looking up at him through her lashes. "I want it rough, Erik. I need you to fuck the violence out of me."

She's speaking words she never thought she'd say, and for one delusional moment, she wonders if she's losing her mind.

But no, it's just her, coming alive after being liberated from the ghosts of her past.

She's finally free.

Her hands work at his belt, and she quickly yanks his pants down, exposing his massive cock to her.

She doesn't even hesitate. Her mouth starts at the tip, and she pushes forward, forcing his length in as deep as he can go.

Erik *roars* and his hands fly to her hair as she works him, sucking him so deeply he hits her gag reflex.

"Fuck, yes," he hisses, thrusting his hips. "Gag yourself on my cock, baby."

A pool of slick gathers between her legs as she sucks him off, one hand working at his shaft while the other fondles his balls. She squeezes hard, a little too rough, and he jerks in her hands.

"If you're going to be difficult, I'm going to have to fuck your mouth," he warns, and she hums around his cock. Without warning, he pushes his hips until her nose meets his stomach and holds her there.

She squirms, her gag reflex kicking in, but he holds her until she starts shaking.

"Never forget who's in charge," he whispers as she struggles. Slick pours out of her, staining the hotel carpet. "Every one of your holes is mine to fuck. For as long as I want."

Her eyes water, and her head swims, and he finally lets her go. She falls to her hands and knees with a sob, a trail of saliva following the tip of his cock to her mouth.

"You're fucking crazy," she hisses, even as her cunt begs for more.

Without warning, he picks her up and tosses her on the bed. "You already knew that, beautiful," he scolds her. "And your pretty little pussy loves it. Now sit on my face."

She doesn't need to be told twice. He lies down on the bed and she lowers her ass to his mouth, watching his cock twitch.

"You don't know how long I've thought about this," he whispers against her core, before gripping her hips and pushing her cunt directly onto his face. He spreads her open with his fingers, licking a thick stripe with his tongue as he feasts on her slick.

Her mouth opens in shock as he suckles on her clit, and she gently rides, careful not to push too hard.

He pauses, his lips leaving her clit, and she cries out from the loss of sensation.

"Don't hold back, baby," he warns, pinching the inside of her thigh. "Ride my face. Bounce on it. I can take it."

So, she does. Drunk on the pleasure, she uses his face, grinding her ass down on him, his tongue invading her. He works her until she's a panting mess, little mews escaping her mouth as she struggles to keep herself upright.

He knows exactly where to lick her. He knows exactly how to suckle on her clit, with a gentle sucking of his lips.

It's ridiculous. It's like he's been with her for years, not days, with the way he expertly pleasures her.

But she wants to return the favor.

His cock, massive and demanding attention, twitches in anticipation. Leaning over, she takes him in her mouth, situating herself over his body. He groans into her cunt as she inhales his scent, then takes him in her mouth as deep as she can. She thrusts on top of him, smothering his face with her cunt, while deep throating his cock.

It's exquisite.

She's coming before she can warn him, and a burst of slick drips from her core, soaking his face. As she moans around him, her throat relaxes, and she feels him inflate.

His knot *inflates in her throat.*

It should be horrifying, but it only spurs her on, as load after load bursts in her mouth.

It's filthy. It creates a mess, and she finally has to release him and suck in air, choking on his seed.

"Holy *fuck,*" he growls into her thigh. "Fuck, baby, are you still coming? Holy *shit.*"

She's barely lucid as she maneuvers off him, gasping for air. Her skin *burns,* the fever from before returning.

She spasms on the blankets as he tends to her.

"Fuck," he hisses, rolling out of bed. She keeps her eyes closed, gyrating helplessly on the mattress, needing *more*.

He returns to her in seconds, a cool cloth wiping at her face and fevered brow.

"I'm going to lose myself soon," he whispers in her ear. "I can't wait much longer. Ellie...I need to claim you."

"Do it," she whispers. "Do it, please. I need it. Fuck me, Erik, *please*."

The cool cloth is gone, and she's lifted higher on the bed. His eyes are wild, full of hunger and dark with need.

Growling, he climbs on top of her and hoists her thigh around his hip. He's torn off his shirt, and her hands wander up his naked chest, her nails leaving scratches in their wake.

He closes his eyes and hisses. "Fuck, yes," he whispers. "Make it hurt, baby."

Then he slams into her and steals the air from her lungs.

He's so *deep*, deeper than before. His knot still inflated, she stretches painfully, whimpering at the ache.

"Good Omega," he hisses, his hips thrusting. "So fucking good for me."

Alpha is pleased!

"More," she begs.

"You want *more*?" He growls, thrusting in harder. "You want me to split this little cunt open?"

She nods, and he works her harder until she's sure she's going to break.

But she needs this. She needs him.

"I love you," she whispers, and he roars.

His teeth are at her gland, and her vision whites out.

CHAPTER 35

ERIK

He wanted to make this last longer, but her words broke him.

The gland breaks easily under his teeth, and her delicious blood fills his mouth. Her life essence tastes even sweeter than her slick, and he moans as he licks at the wound.

His Omega has succumbed to pleasure, her body twitching and spasming, but he's more alert than he's ever been.

The bond connects them, and suddenly she's *everywhere*.

Whatever is left of his heart, the remnants of his soul intertwine with hers, and he feels everything.

He sees her life, the emotions she buries, and the goodness in her heart. Her sorrow and anguish dance through his veins, and he sees many of his own emotions reflected in her.

As he pumps into her, his cum filling her to the brim, he absorbs every stolen memory and secrets she still keeps.

She can't hide from him. Not anymore.

Just like he can't hide from her.

His past is now hers, and she gasps as his emotions tumble into her, his soul melding with her own.

"Mine," he whispers in her ear, his hips slamming against hers. "Your soul is mine, *Omega*."

He swallows her cries of pleasure with his mouth, his tongue plunging into hers deeply, tasting every sweet inch of her mouth.

His Alpha roars, insane with possession and pleasure.

He wants more.

Blood and spit drip from her shoulder as he maneuvers her, rolling them onto their sides. His hand wraps around her throat, pulling her closer to him, as he rocks her on his knot.

"You'll never run from me again, will you?" He snarls at her. "You'll never take this pussy from me again, will you, Omega?"

He hisses filthy demands in her ear, and she chokes out her agreement.

And the little minx likes it. Her cunt drips, and another orgasm takes her as he works her clit into a frenzy. He thrusts once more until his knot is so large and stiff neither of them can move.

He releases her throat, allowing her the sweet pleasure of oxygen, and sucks at her neck.

He continues his ministrations until they both pass out.

———

Her Heat is as violent as his Rut.

She wakes up needy, clawing at his chest until he forces her on her hands and knees, shoving his cock inside her.

This position is different, and he swears he can feel her fucking *womb* as he pounds into her, one hand gripping her hair, forcing her neck back.

"My little *Omega*," he snarls, the beast inside unleashed. "My good girl. You like when your big bad Alpha fucks you?"

She babbles nonsense, and he can barely believe the words that come out of his mouth.

"Gonna breed you, baby. Keep my cum in you until you give me a fucking family."

She *screams*, and her walls clench him impossibly tight. He releases her hair and grabs on to both hips firmly, slamming into her as deeply as he can.

When she's unable to keep herself upright, he bounces her on his lap until she whimpers.

"Alpha," she breathes, and the sound makes his cock twitch.

"Look at me," he snaps, moving her hips up and down with his hands. "Look at me when you come, Ellie."

Her eyes find his, her gaze burning with passion.

"It's always been you," he hisses, working her on his cock. "And always will be you. You're mine. *Forever.*"

He grunts out the last word and she stills, milking every drop of cum out of his body. He roars, a primal, feral sound that shakes the walls.

They collapse together, his arms locked tight around her.

They wake up and do it again.

AFTER WHAT FEELS LIKE DAYS, HER SCENT CHANGES.

Her Heat finally starts to end.

He's taken care of her the best he can when his Rut isn't in overdrive. He fed her, washed her, and kept her tucked into as many blankets as possible.

And of course, he's fucked her senseless.

But she finally stirs, her beautiful face no longer pink from a fever, and she gives him a small smile. "Hi."

"Hey," he responds, smiling back. It's impossible to not smile when his mate is in his arms, and her soul is stamped permanently onto his.

"I think we broke the hotel room," she whispers.

He glances at the damage. There's a hole punched into the wall above the headboard, and a table is flipped over on its side, the chair missing.

"It's fine," he murmurs, kissing the top of her head. "They have a card on file for a reason."

"For 'Mister Jones', right?"

"Sure. Jones, Davis...whoever you want us to be."

She squirms out of his arms and sits up, wrapping a sheet around herself. "You said we would talk," she says quietly. "What does that mean?"

For a moment, anxiety spikes through him.

She's going to try to leave him again.

He's going to have to actually kidnap her.

"It means we discuss our plans," he says slowly. "The ones where we start the rest of our lives."

But to his relief, she smiles, and the bond between them floods with delight. "Well, I have a bit of inheritance left..."

"No." Now it's his turn to sit up. "You don't understand. I could buy this hotel if I wanted to. Hell, I'd buy you a fucking island. It's not about money. It's about what *you* want."

Unless you want to leave me, is the unspoken threat.

But she doesn't seem to hear it, her mind deep in thought, until her eyes narrow in accusation. "You could have left Green Woods years ago," she whispers. "You could have bought Gerard off a long time ago and been in a different country by now. Why didn't you?"

He had asked himself that question before, but he didn't have the answer until he met her.

"I was waiting for something," he replies simply. "I didn't know what it was. I was tempted to leave, but something inside me kept saying to *wait*. Then you showed up."

Her eyes are wide and shiny with disbelief. "You were there for three years," she says.

"The first year, I didn't care," he says. "The first year was awful. They had only found Cassie's body months ago, and I didn't really care what happened to me."

Ellie's pain melds with his, but he forces himself to continue. "But by the second year, I had the entire place mapped out. I knew everything about their security systems because they modeled them after the ones I built. I learned *too* much. I could have left that second year, but there was no place I wanted to be."

He reaches out to squeeze her hand. "Then *you* came along."

Her eyes fall to her lap, and she shifts uncomfortably.

"I don't need to finish the rest of the story."

"No, you don't," she says quietly. "But I've already forgiven you."

He doesn't deserve it, but he still relishes it.

"I meant what I said, though," he continues. "I'm not leaving your side. You're not alone, anymore."

She gives him a small smile, and her love shines through the bond.

"So, where do you want to go?" he asks her.

She smirks, her eyes blazing.

"Surprise me."

EPILOGUE

ELLIE—ONE YEAR LATER

HE HOLDS HER HAND AS SHE LEADS THEM THROUGH THE manicured field, stopping under a large oak tree. The breeze is gentle, a cool wind against her face, as she looks down at the graves. "I haven't been here in years," she murmurs, turning back to look at Erik.

He squeezes her hand in reassurance. "I'm proud of you," he whispers.

She glances at him, his dark eyes gentle. His hair has grown out, falling almost to his shoulders, and his stubble has turned into a full beard.

He doesn't look at all like the face they show on television.

Just like she doesn't look like Ellie Winters.

If anyone asks, they're Audrey and Nathan Wilson, newly-weds visiting from Canada. They live in a quiet town near the border, where Nathan works in IT and Audrey is a stay-at-home wife.

Just a normal couple, like any other.

She can sense the pride Erik has for her, proud that she's found the courage to face her ghosts once again.

"My mom would have liked you," she says suddenly. "But I think my sister would have tried to beat you up."

He chuckles. "I would deserve it."

She quietly observes their graves, grief and longing washing over her.

This is the second phase of their trip.

The first part was stopping to see Cassandra and placing a small bouquet next to her tombstone.

Now, they do the same here; her holding one for her mother, Erik placing one down for her sister.

No one missed Ronald Dennis. They barely mentioned his death in his town's local paper, and only referred to it as a tragic accident.

Apparently, he started a fire in his drunken state, and couldn't make it out in time.

She's free. None of it was pinned on her.

Yet, she chooses to live on the run with Erik, and he does his best to make it up to her.

But the ring on her finger is enough.

Being with him is enough.

Watching him place flowers at his sister's grave is more than enough.

Only Lita knows part of the truth.

I fell in love, she told her. *I'm safe. Will visit eventually.*

Erik squeezes her hand, bringing her back to the present.

"I love you," he tells her quietly. "I wish I could take this pain away from you."

She squeezes his hand back. "You do," she says softly. "Just by being here with me."

He holds her tighter, her soul singing with his, as she reflects on her past.

Everything in her life has led to this moment, where she allows herself to love and be loved. She can finally face her ghosts without fear, with her mate by her side.

She's worthy of being loved. She deserves love.

They're two broken people, but together, they heal.

ABOUT THE AUTHOR

Liliana Carlisle is a romance author that loves angst, drama, and passion. Her characters are always flawed, but almost always redeemable.

She resides in Northern California with her husband, stepchildren, and two emotional cats. She started her writing "career" in seventh grade writing Backstreet Boys fan fiction in her notebooks. When she's not writing she can be found studying classical voice, playing video games, or gulping cold brew coffee.

ALSO BY LILIANA CARLISLE

Made in the USA
Las Vegas, NV
02 October 2023

78473079R00111